ALSO BY

FRANK PICKARD

American Nomad

Island Jewel

Photoplasm: A Haunting

The Weight of Gravity

LUNA

Songs For The Soul

My Haole Brother

PRINCIPAL KEEPER:

A Haunting Love Story

A novel

by

Frank Pickard

And the light shines in the darkness ... John 1:5

Frank Pickard

All rights reserved. Except as permitted under the U.S. Copyright Act of 1976, no part of this publication including text and images may be reproduced, distributed, or transmitted in any form or by any means, or stored in a database or retrieval system, without the prior permission of the author.

www.frankpickard.com

First Edition: January 2021

This story is a work of historical fiction. Stated or implied reference to actual people, living or dead, and events, past or present, depicted in this novel are coincidental and not intended by the author or should be inferred by the reader,.

Cover design by

Sara Jackson Photography

www.sarajacksonphotography.com

Cover Image: Todd Trapani

Prologue

She's not real, but I heard her voice and felt her hand on my face. She wrapped herself around me and I smelled her sweetness. The mist thickened and morphed, and I saw her shadow. She stared in the window, smiled and whispered, and then reached out and begged me to break the glass and hold her.

These memories will haunt me forever.

Decades of time, like the fog, dissipated the moment I set foot on the island. I'm insane, certainly, but she waited a hundred years for me, and then I was there.

It was there, but hardly anyone saw it. When conditions were perfect, a car might pull off onto a high point of the coastal road, the driver step out, lean against the rail, and take a moment to measure its place and prominence, out beyond Fletcher's Point. It was a treat whenever someone saw it, because most days it was hidden in mist, or cloaked in fog. Conditions had to be perfect to see it from shore.

A persnickety lumberman throwing down a short stack and sausages in Delma's Diner one day dared to say out loud, "If it slipped below the waves, it'd be a week before any villager took note."

No one remembered who said it, but no one refuted it. The town folk trusted that it was out there on the water, that it had always been there, always would be, even if you couldn't see it.

"Fog's to blame," they said. Most evenings it hid everything beyond the shore break. Midday the following morning the fog burned away and revealed the village's iconic tourist attraction, the Seward Lighthouse.

Visitors came up from New York in the spring to spend a weekend in one of the inns. You'd see them on the pier staring at the open water. A local with a desire to help stood behind them and stretched an arm over their shoulder, pointed a finger and said, "See, see right there, on the horizon? See that knob, that thing rising out of the water?" Even then, most people could only imagine. It took practice and keen eyesight. "You need to know when and where to look," the local explained. "Mind you, the conditions have to be just right."

The ninety-foot tower of granite and white plaster was three and a half miles from the harbor. At that distance and height, it would be easily visible from land were it not for a persistent haze that gripped the island. It never dissipated. Trade winds and storms only added to the mist that blanketed the lighthouse.

Principal Keeper

Built in 1864, Seward Lighthouse was named for William Seward, Secretary of State under Abraham Lincoln. But it wasn't the Civil War history that interested tourists. Rather, it was a thousand published stories about mysterious activities surrounding the tower and its island.

Seward Lighthouse had a reputation as one of the most haunted sites on the eastern shore. For decades, tales told of unexplained lights, piano music that drifted over the waves and onto the decks of passing ships. In heavy storms, or on cold wintry nights, people reported that they heard a woman crying. The stories took on greater significance when the lighthouse was abandoned and automated in 1973. Ghostly activities persisted well after the last keeper's watch. Although no one lived on the island, mariners still reported they saw a dark figure in a dress on the catwalk outside the lamp house.

Consequently, a steady flow of visitors came to see the Seward each year. To pull in more tourists, villagers told stories of ghostly doings in rooms at the hotels. The spirits of the Seward Lighthouse, it seemed, had come ashore and taken up residence. It wasn't true, but it was good for commerce.

The more affluent paid to be shuttled out for a closer look, but no one was allowed to step onto the rock. Years ago the city council, in coordination with federal authorities, banned site-seeing tours. It was too dangerous for larger boats to ply the choppy waters around the lighthouse. The purpose of the Seward Lighthouse, after all, was to keep ships away from the rocks.

Villagers welcomed outsiders and fostered the quaintness of their New England town. Thoroughfares were widened and Victorian homes were renovated. New business, restaurants and hotels popped up. Images of the lighthouse were everywhere. Miniatures were sold in gift shops, and businesses incorporated the tower into their signage. There was the *Beacon Inn*, the *Lighthouse B&B*, and *Seward's Seafood Diner*. It was common to see a tourist at the height of the season wearing a hat crowned with a stuffed replica of the lighthouse.

Some residents thought the attention was obscene. Others welcomed, and cashed in on the notoriety of their proximity to the mysterious structure.

Most people rarely got a glimpse of it, but I'm cursed. Seward tower, and the crag on which it stood, as well as the keeper's two-storied quarters, and most importantly what lay hidden beneath all of it, will never leave me. I'm chained forever to my memories of life on the island.

This is my story.

Chapter 1

The Tower

It was a short ride from the regional airport along a lonely road that cleaved a forest of spruce and aspen as it weaved through the hills. There was a home, then three, a convenience store and a gas station. Roadside fruit stands were shuttered for the season. Trees parted and the village was there.

The highway cut through the heart of the community, and then climbed the hills to the north, straight on into New England. The harbor was below, and further on we saw the open ocean. It was the color of mercury under an overcast sky.

Bellwether Bay was a thriving fishing port until tourism chased away the fleet of trawlers. Long-time fishers retired or died of old age. Colleges and careers in larger cities lured away the young. Now, no one gave up their lives to un-Godly hours of labor, as their fathers and grandfathers had done, on the cold, dark Atlantic waters.

I learned that villagers explained all things, good and bad, with a dismissive, "it's Bellwether Bay, now, isn't it?" Someone might say, "Gonna have a hard rain today," and another would respond, "it's Bellwether Bay, now, isn't it." You got the same response if you commented on the lovely holiday decorations around town. The quip was short and simple, and helped to end any weighty explanation.

We drove to the pier and I boarded the launch. Inboard engines thundered, twin props churned beneath the gunwale, and we plied away from the dock and through the tide, out into the harbor.

Our destination was thirty minutes out, but we didn't see it until we were nearly halfway there. It rose like the Colossus of Rhodes, lamp held up to torch the clouds.

This was my new home.

Based on appearance, it was a typical and ordinary lighthouse that resembled the dozens of others in the northeast, built on desolate slips of rock, apart from the mainland and accessible only by water. The beacon at Bellwether Bay was more isolated than most.

When I visited the lighthouse the first time, the launch captain maneuvered the boat close enough to drop me onto the island. Waves broke over the rocky shoreline. There seemed no safe landing until he circled ocean side, throttled the engine, and let the waves push us against a slab of concrete with a slip of sand beneath the pylons.

The tower loomed over me. Forest green portals spaced every eight feet rose up the white walls, and marked the progress of the spiral staircase inside. Halfway up was a metal door and an iron balcony large enough for a single person to stand and survey the ocean. A steel catwalk with brass railings rimmed the lamp house. A brass-plated frame encased the prism. A burnished copper cupola at the top capped it all.

The keeper's quarters were landward, twenty yards beyond the tower. The granite foundation and stonewalls were whitewashed, and window frames were painted to match the portals on the tower.

As he'd done before, the boatman tossed a deck line over a pylon and pulled the starboard side of his boat against the pier. He held it fast while I jumped onto the dock, then he spun the wheel and throttled into the waves. He growled when a swell threw him back toward the rocks, but pushed it forward, looped to circle the island and then headed back to Bellwether Bay.

I pulled the coat against my shoulders and raised the collar. Leaden clouds raced overhead and toppled the tower down on me. I felt dizzy. The rock crumbled beneath my feet. I was two-dimensional, a lone figure in a painting of blue skies, greens and white plaster. In truth, we're insignificant, my tower and me, captured between a rising ocean and a falling sky, It's beautiful, much like a McKnight painting in color and composition. Like the ones my wife hung in our upper West Side apartment, and at our home in White Plains.

I'd come to live in a surreal, amorphous world, alone, just as I desired, just as I planned. It fed a yearning, a need for solitude. I stood alone on a citadel surrounded by leviathan waves and the

11

shrillness of gale-force winds that can't decide which way to throw me to the ground. These are my companions. This impenetrable stone and tower has weathered nature for a hundred years. Its survival matched my resolve to live and work here.

During my first visit to Seward Lighthouse, I was given a tour of the living quarters and received instructions on the operation of the lamp and foghorn. They were automated decades ago, but never proved dependable. Service crews came to the remote outpost to make repairs.

"But here's the strange thing," the Park Service supervisor said to me that day. "We never found anything wrong with the equipment. We'd reset the system, fire it up, and everything operated fine. Weird, right?" He wiped his nose with his sleeve. "A month later we'd be back doing it all over again."

"Maybe there are ghosts on the island," I told him. "I read literature in Bellwether Bay ..."

"Nonsense," he interrupted. "That talk is all hooey to get tourists to drive up and spend a week dropping money all over town. You don't believe any of that silliness the locals spin about the lighthouse, do you?"

"Of course not," I told him.

"Good, 'cuz this here's a big deal, putting you on this rock. The only folks living in lighthouses anymore bought them and turned them into personal residences. Only one lighthouse in our system still has a paid keeper. Boston Harbor. The decision to hire you to keep watch out here took a lot of wrangling in the home office. I'd be a shame if you got spooked and jumped ship now."

"Being the keeper for the Seward Lighthouse fits perfectly into my plans," I told him. "Ghosts or no ghosts, I won't be coming back to the mainland."

"Good to hear," he said and continued our tour.

The instructions that day were heavy on "Don't let this happen in a storm," and "Here's the proper tool to use," before an unceremonious, "Here be the keys."

My final lesson that day came from the boat captain who gave us a ride back to Bellwether Bay.

"So you're the new keeper," he announced.

"Looks that way," I said, and stared up at the tower as we pulled away.

"I were a keeper once," he said, and spit over the side into the waves. "Got a bit o'thoughts to share," he said. "Be mindful the temperament of the sea-maid whar'er she cast her eyes, young fellow. Do ya hear me?"

He reminded me of a classic movie with Errol Flynn shouting at his crew to *trim the mainsail and batten the hatches, cuz it'll be a long night and weary journey, me maties.*

I looked at the government official. He smiled. "Listen to what he has to say," he told me. "It's good advice."

"I hear you," I said to the captain.

"Aye, but do ye understand the meaning of m'words?"

13

"I suppose so," I said.

"Er'ye been on a rock a'for," he asked.

"No, I haven't," I answered.

"No, I din't think so. Well, ther'ant nothin' like 'em." He turned his furrowed face to look back at the tower. He fingered the buttons on his tweed coat, and hunkered lower into the collar.

I wondered if someday I'd be as weathered as the captain. The old man was salted and bent. Hard labor in unforgiving elements left him scarred and broken.

"Were you a keeper on an island, Mr. Hobbs?" I asked.

"'Rocks,' we called 'em, along the Irish coast. Trinity House were the gov'ment's administration for all the lights, for over two hun'erd ye'rs," he said. "I started on a peninsula, but was the youngest PK in Trinity's history and youngest to ev'r get assigned rock duty."

I thought he'd finished. He swept his hand down his face from forehead-to-chin, as though he was smoothing out the wrinkles. Then said, "I stayed out there for nineteen ye'r until they forced me to take s slow shallow on the land."

"So you have a long history of lighthouse work," I said.

"How long we'r ye an APK?" he asked.

"I was never an assistant keeper," I told him.

"Gaw," he said, then spit chaw over the side into the wake. Bits of the dark liquid slid down the railing and onto the deck. "We did a min'mum twelve ye'r in my day a'for you made PK." He squinted one eye and threw the other one onto me.

"I'm impressed that you were the youngest principal keeper in the Trinity House service, Mr. Hobbs," I said.

He snarled and grunted. "Most were not 'er lucky as me, that's all."

He was silent for the remainder of the trip back to the harbor.

His words and stare came back to me, as I stood alone on the island. The weight of my decision to take this job settled on my shoulders. It was cold and windy, and damp to the point of being uninhabitable. Such circumstances could, in time, bend and break a person.

That conversation was a month ago. My only contact now was a satellite phone, a landline when it was working, and a CB radio to the harbormaster, if all else failed. Every two weeks someone delivered provisions and anything else I requested. They advised me to take a break every couple months, and visit Bellwether Bay. Once each year, someone relieved me and I could take a two-week vacation.

All of this was at my discretion. I didn't have to do any of it. My duties were to trouble-shoot the glitch-y equipment, to make certain it operated properly. That didn't require anyone else's assistance. It was a one-man show, and that suited me fine.

Chapter 2

It was seventy paces from the steel door of the tower to the keeper's house. Most of the island was visible from the catwalk. In fair weather, which was rare, a person might see the shadow of the shoreline and harbor of Bellwether Bay.

I took stock in the moment. Going forward for years to come, this desolate place was home. I wasn't disillusioned. I knew it'd take time to acclimate. Choppy seas, high winds and frequent storms were common this far north. Those were givens. I had only to grow comfortable with the isolation, of listening to voices in my head, seeing my reflection in the mirror, and with no one to greet me each morning when I started my duties. I'd read stories of lost souls at sea, alone, drifting for days or months. They'd go crazy, shout at the moon, hallucinate unimaginable things, and then jump into the water and disappear. They left journals that documented their madness. I didn't plan to drift that far from reality.

I'd guard against such things. I'd start a hobby: maybe woodcarving or stargazing. I'd journal, just as I'd done for most of my life. I'd read, and write a novel. Maybe paint or take up photography, but that'd be ridiculous since little changed on the island, with the exception of the weather. And that was either fair or foul, depending on the season.

With that thought, a colony of seagulls flew overhead, gawked and squawked, and made their presence known. They mocked me, shouting that they were the only true inhabitants of this place, and I was an unwelcomed visitor.

The keys to the main house, foghorn shanty and the tower were in a safe in the kitchen cabinet. It seemed absurd that anything needed to be locked. I was told that on occasion an uninvited visitor, or a gaggle of rowdy teenagers from the village, would attempt to visit the island, but the chance of them safely coming ashore were slim.

Storms were frequent and sudden, so it was risky to moor a boat to the tiny pier. If someone did come ashore and a nor'easter rolled in, they could find themselves living on the island for a week or more, until the waves and wind grew calm, and a boat picked them up.

There'd be no casual drop-ins. That was a comforting thought. There'd be weeks in the winter when I'd be isolated until warmer seas returned. I was anxious for the dark days. I craved solitude and silence. It'd be an existence of a different dimension from my former life. I understood, now, how someone's world could turn upside down. The weight of things can unexpectedly pull your north to the south, and south becomes normal.

Frank Pickard

I felt the mist. I tasted brine. I dropped my things in the largest bedroom at the end of the hall and headed for the tower.

Chapter 3

Settling In

A clunky padlock and heavy key opened the door. Layers of forest green paint softened the rivets. Paint, I was told, was protection against rust.

"Exposed iron will rust overnight out here," the superintendent said during our tour. "If ya get rust, then you gotta sand the metal, slab it with naval jelly, and throw a thick coat of paint on it. Don't matter much what color." He looked around. "Green and white is popular here, as ya can see."

The hinges were well oiled. The dungeon-like door opened easily. The floor of the tower was flagstone. A four-by-four platform with rebar embedded in the concrete was in the middle of the room. In another age, it anchored pulleys used to raise equipment to the top.

I paused at each portal to survey the landscape as I walked up the steps. It'd be useful to know which direction a ship was approaching in a squall. At the top were a ladder and a trap door in the floor of the lamp room. A metal-framed glass door led onto the balcony, called the gallery. It ringed the glass-enclosed lamp housing.

The view stole my breath. The coastline to the west stretched north and south of Bellwether Bay, and was pocked with a labyrinth of nooks and bays, craggy out-cropping and coves. It was landscape carved thousands of years ago by a mile-high shelf of glacial ice. Every channel along the coast was notched with shoals, granite shelves, and islands.

The rest of the world beyond the shores of the island was an unending expanse of water: choppy and dark, deep, cold and speckled with whitecaps. It was hard to imagine a more isolated existence. Roughly fifteen miles to the southeast, a cargo ship inched closer to the Mainland, probably headed to the Red Hook Terminal in New York. In another life I had reason to know the details of the container operations at Red Hook. Those days are gone.

I'd take a day or two to settle into the living quarters and establish a routine of duties. Too, I wanted to study how my new world changed from dawn to dusk, how light and darkness washed over the landscape. Perhaps I'd start a garden. Within the week, I'd begin to take excursions to explore the island. It was nearly a mile long, half a mile wide, with hardly a stick of vegetation, although a trio of tall pines to the southeast lauded over a sixty-foot, sheer drop to the rocks and waves below. I'd noticed the trees from the water on my two trips out.

I stepped outside that first evening and stood in awe of a night sky that brimmed with stars. I'll order a telescope, I decided, and mount it on the tower catwalk. The lens would reach beyond the lamplight, and bring me closer to the heavens.

Stars were nearly nonexistent when I lived in the City. Now, on the path between the tower and residence, I stared up into a canopy glutted with tightly packed pinpoints of light. I felt small, a mere pencil point in the middle of the ocean. I took a deep breath, swelled my chest and put my hands in my pockets.

My island, I thought, *my island and my tower*.

My eyes climbed the white walls that stretched into darkness until the explosion of light at the top.

I was excited, but uncertain why. This was a new adventure, a unique challenge to live alone on an island. I'd found a place and purpose that promised to bring me peace of mind after an incredibly turbulent year.

I walked to the residence and heard rustling in the rafters above the doorway.

Seagulls nesting in the overhangs, I thought. *I'll check on it at first light.*

I slept well, given the unfamiliar surroundings and well-worn bed. I grabbed a peach, a second cup of coffee and headed out.

I looked up when I stepped outside, but there were no fowl in the eaves. Perhaps they roosted only at night. A flock of gulls, however, were gathered on the grass in front of the tower. They were unperturbed when I approached, as though they'd accepted me.

Once inside the tower, I went to the crown and stepped out onto the balcony. The thunder of the waves striking the rocks below was theme music for the world around me. The birds took flight, and circled the tower. They hovered in midair, a foot from my grasp. I wanted to lean out and touch their wings. Three came to settle on the cupola above me. There was a ladder. I'd muster more courage before I climbed it. A lightening rod and weather vane at the apex would require attention one day. I was still leery of the height, as I stood at the railing. I'd wait until I was accustomed before I ventured higher.

I circled the lamp room and sorted my thoughts. Here I would write and read and sleep and eat in my own time, at my own pace. I'd start a new life so different from the one I left behind. It was a blank canvas defined by compass points and bright lights that searched the darkness. It was fitting, I thought, that the beacon of the tower had, in a way, guided me home, to a new home with a new reality. The bricks were stacked, the mortar was mixed and moist, and I was eager to begin rebuilding my life.

I had kinship with the tower. Its powerful beam was there to guide me into safe harbor. I felt renewed and stood strong against the

Principal Keeper

railing. I'd embrace life on the island, imprisoned and isolated by the sea.

I made the rounds and ran the equipment through their checklists. The afternoon sun waned and gave way to gray sky. An undersea cable had long ago replaced the oil lamps in the caretaker's house, but I preferred the shadows. I ate dinner under a single bulb over the kitchen table. The yellow light rose to the rafters and spread softly around the room.

It was my first big meal, a memorable feast to commemorate the occasion. I fried a thick piece of ham, and garnished it with gravy and a sweet dill-mustard sauce. I baked black sourdough biscuits. Wine completed the main course. Blue cheese and Portuguese honey-loaf bread was dessert.

I rested back and took stock of the quarters. In earlier times, two keepers manned the lighthouse: a principal and an assistant. Occasionally these men were married and had children, so the house was large enough to accommodate, with a sitting room, parlor and four bedrooms. There was a large pantry since provisions were stocked to feed everyone for a month or two. Behind the house, accessible through a narrow door from the kitchen, was a storeroom. It contained rain gear, oil canisters and coalscuttles, lash lines, chains, paint and tools. There were stands of wood for repairs, like on the roof of the home. There was also a welding rig.

Besides the kitchen, there was a sitting area to the left of the front door where I'd keep personal reading materials. An office

23

space was to the right. There was a desk and chair with ledgers and logs, but I'd use this space for my own writing, as well. There was a bookshelf stocked with manuals on government policy and equipment repair. The CB radio was for communicating with the harbormaster, receiving messages, and to call the Coast Guard in emergencies.

A stone fireplace with a thick mantel festooned with nautical bric-a-brac was to the right of the desk.

Narrow stairs along the south wall led to the second floor and the bedrooms, only one of which had furniture. The single bathroom had a claw-foot tub and a porcelain sink.

Everywhere I turned there were vestiges of the old with the new. A home of this age, and so far from the mainland and the rest of the world, was bound to retain some of the original elements, things that stood the rigors of time.

I ate the last of the sweet bread, filled my cup with wine, and set out to check the lamp and enjoy the night view of the ocean from the tower.

I could hardly see the water, but I heard the breakers. I counted the conning lights on freighters that inched along the horizon. I felt at peace. I thought about storms that raged and railed over the island, and wondered when they'd come again.

I saw it then, below, a soft light. It was in my peripheral vision one moment, then gone. Maybe the wine was playing with my mind. Then it was there, again, a white glow on the stone pier. I knew about luminescent fish and mysterious lights such as St. Elmo's fire. But those things came during lightning storms. It disappeared again.

Had to be the fish, I decided.

I checked the timers that triggered the lamp and foghorn, and I tripped alarm breakers that let me know when the systems malfunctioned. Everything was good.

I headed back to the house. I'd slept well my first night, listening to the waves, with a full belly and a wine buzz. I expected to have another restful evening.

Chapter 4

Settling In

The first week was monotonous. No storms or equipment failures. I never tired of hearing the waves, and I didn't miss human contact. I spent a lot of time at the railing on the tower balcony staring out at the ocean. I imagined the island was a ship and the tower was a mast, and the balcony was a crow's nest. Clouds passing overhead made it appear as though I was plowing through the waves.

I shouted at the wind, and spoke to myself as I went about my business.

"Don't forget to reset the wind gauge on the foghorn shanty," I reminded myself one day. "Keep the rain meters dry."

I started a journal as a first step to writing my own story. A satellite link provided Internet access, so I started a computer file of my thoughts, but eventually I wrote in long hand. I even used a classic fountain pen I found in the desk drawer. It felt old school, and reminded me of my undergraduate days.

When I thought it might get boring, something interesting occurred. It began with the journal. While writing about my day, I wrote *"down below"* for no reason. I was in the middle of a sentence and it popped out, as though my stream of consciousness had been hijacked. I crossed through the words, and went on to finish my entry.

Two days later I wrote, *"Found gulls nesting in the shanty eaves. Decided to leave them alone. Didn't want them to ..."* I meant to write, *"... be with nowhere to lay their eggs,* but instead I wrote, *"Didn't want them to ... drown."* Drown? Where did that come from, I wondered? I scratched through the word and corrected it.

The equipment malfunctions I was warned about began a week later, always at night. The alarms signaled that the lamp was out and I'd raced from a warm bed out into the cold. But, every time, the light was still burning. It was a simple task to reset the breaker panel, but it still pissed me off.

When enough days passed to set my mind at ease, the alarm would sound again and force me out into the night, only to find that there was nothing wrong with the lamp. I'd go into the tower, up the spiral stairs and check the setting on the mechanism, but I never found anything to explain it.

I thought moisture might be shorting out the wires, because the malfunctions were always in the evening when temps were low and fog rolled across the island. So I spent a day cleaning the contacts, installing new clips and replacing anything that had rust on it.

All was good for nearly two weeks and then it happened again. The alarm rang, I rushed out in my boots, no socks, rain slicker over my jams, and into the tower. I spiraled to the top of the stairs, through the door and opened the panel under the lamp. Nothing, as usual, was amiss. Everything was functioning properly. I stepped out onto the balcony to look for the lights of night trawlers and tankers. I counted three. Then I saw it, the light below the tower. Fog passed over a three-quarter moon, and I saw the shape of a person, a women in a long dress. She stood at the end of the pier, turned and looked up at me, and then she was gone.

I was stunned. There was no logical explanation. Perhaps the moonlight and fog were playing tricks. Or it was pareidolia, when your mind pulls random stimuli together to see what doesn't exist. Like seeing a face in tree bark, or animals in the clouds, or a portrait of a loved one in your burnt toast. Absurd, I know, but I didn't have an answer for what I saw on the dock.

The next morning I was convinced that whatever I saw from the tower was too far away to see clearly. It was farfetched to think it was an apparition, and more logical to believe a natural phenomenon materialized in the darkness to play with my mind.

I was tired of the false alarms. The reset panel was outside the tower door. I knew that the government inspector wouldn't approve, but I trenched and ran a second line to a spot on the wall inside the keeper's house, next to the coat rack. I could see the tower from the window, so next time I heard the alarm, I'd check to make certain the lamp was still shining, and reset the circuit without leaving the warmth of the house.

"Mustn't get too comfortable with that," I told myself when I finished the wiring and tested it.

A month passed with no strange lights on the shore below the tower. The false alarms ceased, as though my rewiring the breaker fixed the issue. I got into a habit of going to the tower in the evening, before turning in for the night.

I grew comfortable with the height, and found a ledge a few feet below the apex of the mantel, on the skirt of the cupola. The powerful light beneath me reached beyond the place where ocean met sky. It spanned the universe to light a distant star. I sat in the center of everything, the lone inhabitant, and my light was the only illumination on my tiny planet. It was a guidepost to the heavens and all the stars and all the travelers.

Then one day I received a radio call from the Coast Guard weather service that warned me that conditions over the next thirty-six hours favored the development of a storm front. Finally, I thought, after weeks of diligent maintenance on the equipment, I'd be rewarded with a major storm, perhaps a raging squall. All the attention I'd given to cleaning the mantel, adjusting the lamp, testing the foghorn, there'd now be a chance to use these tools for the purpose they were designed.

Thirty hours later, nothing had changed. I was tense, on guard, ready to jump into action. I'd laid out my orange and yellow slicker, Wellies and rain cap with the chinstrap.

But the sky was blue and clear. The clouds were wispy and languid, and in no particular hurry to devolve into stormy weather. By nightfall of the second day, I began to question the accuracy of the report.

"It's a prediction. Nothing more," I told myself. "Guess work, at best."

I was on the balcony until eleven before I retired to read a chapter in my novel, fill a page in my journal, and then head to bed. I was perturbed when I spilt water on my journal. The ink on the opposite page bled through and soiled the line I was writing. I stopped, turned out the light and headed upstairs.

In my dreamscape, I'm in a hallway of the New York trading company where I worked. Everyone is staring. They're angry. Their mouths are open, they're shouting, but I can't hear them. They shove me and block the elevator doors.

I wake and sit up. I'm covered in sweat, as usual. A storm is pounding the walls and the alarm in the hallway is blaring. It's time to go to work.

Stonewalls rattled under the force of the wind and rain. The floor vibrated, as did the cabinets, bookshelves and tables.

Most frightening, was the sound. The peaceful lull of the waves was swamped by a monstrous howl and groan, like metal

Principal Keeper

beams pulling against their rivets. The wind blew through the rafters and buffeted the windows. The scream grew from a mournful wail to the bone-ripping cry of a banshee.

I closed the wooden shutters in case the glass shattered. There were baffles in the attic that released the pressure so that the house didn't explode from the inside out.

I dressed in heavy gear, and hesitated before I threw the latch and opened the door. The wind and rainwater threw me back into the room. I leaned my shoulder into it, pushed through the door and closed it behind me.

I grew up in the Midwest. I was familiar with the wind and rain of a tornado. This was similar, but a Northeastern squall was different, unpredictable. I felt as though I'd be blown across the rocks and into the water. It struggled to walk a straight line to the tower.

The flashlight illuminated the rainfall better than it lit the path. It was useless until I got into the tower.

The growl of twisting steel was more intense here. There was no wind, but the sound outside was deafening. I climbed to the top and through the trap in the floor of the lamp house. It felt as though the tower were rocking side-to-side. I slipped out onto the balcony, and held tight to the rail. The slicker whipped against my shoulders, the rain hat flew off and hung by the strap around my neck. When the wind subsided and the rain fell vertically along the tower walls, I scanned the darkness for conning lights moving in the channel. If

31

their great engines failed, they'd be pushed onto the rocks, and I'd be calling the Coast Guard to evacuate the crew.

I saw nothing, or heard any distress signals. Ships in danger would launch flares, but there was none of that. I'd to return to the house and radio the mainland to ask if the harbormaster had any scheduled arrivals on her log.

I used all my strength to open the door to the lamp house. I worried it would slam against my arms and hands. Broken bones received no medical attention until calmer weather prevailed.

I opened the trap and began to descend when a faint glow out beyond the tower caught my eye. It was a good mile away, and gone as quickly as it came. Then it was there again, faint, and pulsing bluish-green. It glowed, out above the waves. I thought it moved toward the island. Then it was gone.

Perhaps it was an errant buoy marker and the steel plates on its scaffold reflected the lamplight each time it cycled round. Or a climatic phenomenon, like ball lightning, or 'St. Elmo's fire', which were common in rainstorms over the ocean.

The shore operator patched me through to the harbor watch who confirmed that no ships were scheduled to arrive before noon. By then, as predicted, the storm will have passed.

The days following dawned gray and chilly. There was a change in the air, a shift in light and temperature. I smelled it and felt it on my skin. The sky was milky. Sunlight was so diffused that it was difficult to know precisely where the sun hung in the sky. The fall and winter months announced their arrival to the northern coastline, and I was settled in my new home and prepared for the storm season.

A week of rain followed before Indian summer returned. Fair weather meant I had time to prepare. The violent storm was a teaser, a warning, and a precursor of things to come. The harbormaster told me as much when I complained about the storm.

"Y'h'aint seen a good'en yet," the radio voice said. "Jes wait't ya get some of that warm gulfstream up here bangin' against the Artic freeze. Then yu'll know what a real storm's 'bout."

"Can't wait," I told him.

His words were troubling, a bit, but I welcomed the change of pace. I cherished solitude and was annoyed when the old man who brought me to the island returned one day to stock my provisions.

"Don't know when I'll have a chance to come agin," he told me. "Best I bring these things now 'afor the storm season git's a goin'."

I was pleased to see his boat depart. I felt ownership with the island, and I didn't like the thought of sharing it with anyone.

Piddling rain fell an hour later. I'd begun to read weather patterns. Harder rain would follow, I predicted. I liked learning to read the signs, as though I had a hand in creating it all.

Chapter 5

The wind gusted. By dinnertime, rain battered the walls. The harbormaster radioed to say that two freighters planned to skirt the storm and push for safe harbor. After I cleared the table, I went to the tower with binoculars and began my vigil.

The first ship passed four miles out, and was safe in port when the wind began to howl and lash the island. Light was dying, but I stayed and searched the horizon for the second vessel. The harbormaster would call when it arrived dockside, or let me know that the captain decided to fight the storm further out. I repeatedly looked for the flashing red light on the east wall of the house that signaled a call was waiting.

I couldn't remember being out in a storm for such a long time. I was dry in my slicker, boots and cap, but my muscles ached and my eyes burned from the strain to see through the mix of hail, wind and rain.

Then, there it was in my binoculars: a single light on the deck, then a second and third. The ship made steady progress. The crew had to be concerned they'd lose control and their ship would be torn apart before lashing dockside. They wanted to get home where it was warm, dry and safe. I felt the rapid beat of their hearts from my lofty perch.

"Come on, you fool!" I said out loud.

I followed the pinpoints of light until I was distracted by a glow off to the left. It was the same bluish-green light I'd seen before. With no lightning, I couldn't dismiss it as a weather phenomenon. I couldn't judge, at first, whether the mysterious glow moved toward or away from the rocks. I didn't see a source until it came closer. Then I thought I saw a figure before it dissipated. I waited for it to reappear, but it didn't.

An hour passed. The freighter was moored in the harbor, and I left my post and retired to the quarters.

Sleep was impossible. It wasn't my habit to stay in bed after first light, but I had serious thoughts. Where did the unexplained light come from, and why did I only see it during storms? Surely there was a connection, and an explanation.

A week passed, and then another. The routine returned and I stopped fixating on the mysterious lights. I kept vigil for several hours each night on the catwalk, but the air was still, and the clouds high and dry, except for a veil of virga on the northern horizon.

With a cup of coffee cradled in my palms, and leaned against the brass railing high above the shoreline, I thought about Central Park, the leaves, the quilting of fall colors that framed my suburban home in White Plains. I thought about walks under the arbor along

35

the path behind my home. I smelled sweet smoke from the wood stoves and fireplaces. I pulled my collar high and buried my hands in a cashmere waistcoat: a Christmas gift from my wife that year.

These were good memories, filled with pleasant thoughts of a time before events changed my life, and chased me to this island.

My life was complex then, and cluttered with worn habits and throwaway thoughts. I had a lucrative job as a Wall Street executive, and was married to a beautiful lawyer with her own practice. Life was pleasant, full of material things and glittery holiday parties where career-absorbed business associates paraded their significant others around the room. We all had hefty bank accounts, growing stock portfolios, and limitless futures.

That was my life.

Then it all changed. Now I occupied a solitary, desolate outpost in a remote and inhospitable corner of the planet. The landscape had changed, but I wasn't complaining.

Perched on the tower with my collar raised to brace against the chill, I thought about these things. They were memories of a different place and a life left in shadows.

A few mild fronts came and passed in the weeks after. Stronger storms were just beyond the horizon. I'd need to stay prepared.

I sank back into a familiar, comfortable routine. One morning I walked the mile-long circumference of the rocky shore. On the west end of the island, nearest to the mainland, I found the cliff I'd

Principal Keeper

seen from the water. I stood at the top. The slope dropped directly into the waves, sixty feet below. There was no path down to the bottom, and the rocks kept anyone from coming close in a boat.

Three Jack pines grew clustered along the ledge. It was a place to sit in the shade and enjoy the smells of the ocean enriched by the sugary scent of warm pine needles. I'd bring a stool next time and tie it to a tree so it didn't blow off the cliff. It would be a respite, an escape from my labors. I'd come here to think and write. I was a monk, cloistered and sworn to vows of silence and meditation. This place suited deep thoughts, beneath the pines, high above the waves. This corner of the island would be a vacation from the tower.

I didn't know, as I headed back to the lighthouse, that everything I knew about the island was about to change.

Chapter 6

The Discovery

I thought little of the cliff and pine trees until an accident a week later led to an amazing discovery. I planned to spend the day polishing the brass fixtures on the tower. They tarnished easily in storms and the hot sun. It wasn't a good idea to let them get too dull before scrubbing the metal with a mixture of salt, flour and vinegar. It brought back the luster and protected the brass.

My arms were full with polishing paste, a bucket, rags, and a final cup of morning tea when I started up the tower stairs. I took five steps and dropped my teacup. The liquid spilled onto the stone floor.

My first thought was that I hated wasting good tea on a cold morning. Then I witnessed something mysterious. The tea evaporated into the floor. It was there, and then gone, as though the stone was a sponge.

I stepped back, set down the cleaning materials and kneeled where the tea hit the floor. I touched the stone. It was dry. Perhaps the mortar between flagstones was aged and porous, I thought. That made sense. I picked up the bucket and poured water onto the floor. It funneled under the concrete slab. There was a cavity beneath the floor, below the platform with the rebar anchors. I'd report it to the supervisors. Maybe there was erosion under the tower. A work crew would come and assess the problem, and fix it.

Weather held calm. Conditions were poised for heavy seas, harsh rain and high winds. Regardless of the earlier storms, the best were to come. I took weekly ocean temperature readings. The water was cooler, the waves were darker, and they broke on the rocks with greater urgency. These were signs of bigger storms on the horizon. An advance army of young soldiers tested the battlements with whitecaps and icy waters before the larger force of seasoned fighters came ashore.

That's how it felt.

I wasn't concerned. I'd match my weapons and myself against whatever the sea and nature brought. I was anxious for a northeaster. The late summer storms whetted my appetite for battle.

Three days passed before the sky darkened. I rose one morning to find the clouds bubbling and rolling above the tower. The damp air was palpable. There was no wind, but the fog was thick. I tripped the breaker on the foghorn. Its deep-throated voice buffered through the mist. The calm was unsettling as I began my rounds. Sunlight failed to break through to burn away the gray. The weather worsened. By noon, the island was saturated in fog and the calm was

39

deafening. The air was charged, poised for action. A breeze teased the windsock above the storage shed. I stared at it until it stirred again.

I heard the bell and saw the red light flashing. The harbormaster was calling.

"Batten your hatches," were the first words I heard through the radio.

"Storm coming?" I asked.

"Big storm coming, fella', no doubt about it. Your own instruments are spiking jus' about now."

I looked at the barometer above the desk. It had dropped eight points since last I recorded the readings. Humidity was higher.

"How soon should I expect the storm?" I asked.

"Jus' expect you'll have a sleepless night," he added.

"Any ships coming through?"

I heard his cough before he said, "Only the Ebenezer June, but she's due 'afor it's all to start. They'll be moored tight in two hours." There was a long pause. "Keep yer' head low, the lamp burning and windows locked. We'll get back to ya in the dawn's light to check how it's going."

The wind gusted and bullied me when I stepped outside. There was no doubt. It'd be a major blow, but I was confident, ready for the fight. I'd felt this type of wind before, in New York. It was strong enough to blow away one season and usher in the next.

Conditions worsened. I'd check the alarms one last time before I retreated to the cottage to wait out the storm.

I watched the conning lights of the 'Ebenezer June' pass the harbor markers. The weather stations were functioning well when I headed in for dinner. The wind howled and rattled the shutters. The despondent foghorn called out for lost souls. The storm gathered strength. I ran through the scenarios of what I would do if the lights or the horn failed. No ships were out there, but not every vessel reported their position. There could be a private yacht or schooner.

This was the moment I prepared for, the challenge that would test my training. Feelings of isolation were a given on the island, but it was absolute in these moments. I was alone and unreachable. I was buried under the darkness as the storm's intensity grew. This would test and temper me. It was time.

I sat tight. I didn't need to rush out if the equipment was functioning properly. If there were no alarm bells and the foghorn bellowed, then all was well.

Still, I was restless. Rain lashed the walls. Earlier, after the weather report, I ran a line of quarter inch cable from the cottage to the tower. I had the idea weeks ago during a mild rainfall. I stepped out onto the porch and grabbed the cable. Waves spilled over the rocks along the path. I pulled myself along, hand-over-hand. I saw the tower door and the light above it. I looked up to the top of the tower. The raindrops stung my face.

I was thrown against the metal door. I turned the latchkey and tumbled into the tower. I rose, closed the door and headed up the stairs. The walls groaned and the stairs shuttered. Sheets of rainwater clouded the windows, as though I were under water.

The tower rumbled as I approached the top. I reminded myself that it had stood strong for over a hundred and fifty years. Someday the storms would win and throw the tower into the sea, but hopefully that wouldn't be on my watch. Not tonight.

I passed through the trap door and into the mantel room. I was surrounded by the storm. The thick glass separated me from the monster. Wind and rain hammered the tall window. I didn't dare risk stepping out onto the balcony. The bulwark held fast against my enemy. As long as the light burned, my private island universe was secure.

There was nothing for me to do, so I decided to retreat to the safety of the cottage. As I approached the bottom of the spiral stairs, I felt fear. Inextricably, a wave of anxiety washed over me and chilled my blood. My heart raced. There was danger in the shadows.

I got to the bottom and hesitated at the door. I put the flashlight in my pocket so that I could grasp the cable with both hands the moment I stepped outside. I listened to the storm beyond the doorway. I turned out the lights in the room, and stood in pitch darkness, with the exception of the flashes of lightning in the ports above. Chilled air blew through the room. There was no source, no open window or door. It came from the darkness beneath the stairs.

Principal Keeper

Only then did I see it. A bluish-green glow seeped through the edges of the flagstone pedestal. The light moved along the circular walls as though the source were moving beneath the stone. It was the same light I'd seen before, from the balcony. Now, it was somewhere below the tower, and it was alive.

I threw open the door and rushed out. I grabbed the cable and pulled myself along until I stood at the cottage. I went in and bolted the door behind me. I took the steps three at a time to the second floor, ran down the hallway and sat in the chair in the corner of the room, next to my bed. I stared at the open doorway, and all the way down the hall. I heard my breathing and saw my breath. The lights flickered. Shadows filled the corners. I stared at the oval mirror on the opposite wall, above the dresser. It was dark.

I leaned forward, fixed my eyes at the doorway and waited, but nothing happened. I was slumped in the chair when sunlight came through the curtains and hit my eyes.

For a moment, I felt peaceful, but then I realized that it hadn't been a dream. The mysterious glow below the tower was real and searching for me.

Chapter 7

The storm died. I was stiff and achy when I stood and walked into the hallway. I felt exhausted. Sunlight burned my eyes when I stepped out into the yard. The ground was littered with seaweed, driftwood and foamy puddles.

I opened the door to the tower and my eyes went directly to the stone platform in the middle of the room. I stepped in, crouched down and felt the edge where the concrete met flagstone. A cool breeze escaped from the crack. I took a bladed screwdriver from a tool cabinet and chiseled at the rock. A half-hour later, I opened a space large enough to insert a crowbar and leverage the stone up and to the side. I stared into a narrow shaft that dropped ten feet below the floor of the tower. Rusted metal rungs were embedded in the rock wall. It was a means to climb down into the well. The light in the tower dimmed as I dropped further into the hole.

At the bottom of the shaft was an opening that led to a narrow horizontal tunnel. I could see the end, but it appeared to descend deeper underground. I imagined a dark, sinister form coming out of the darkness toward me.

Principal Keeper

The tunnel was damp and cold. As I climbed back up into the base of the tower, I noticed that the walls of the well were damp. Tidewater must have surged into the tunnel during the storm, I thought. Somewhere, this well opened to the sea.

I walked out into the sunlight. My curiosity was peaked. So, I tightened the laces on my boots, grabbed a sealed-beam flashlight from the tool shed and headed back to the tower. I climbed down into the hole, clicked on the lamp and started down the tunnel.

Twenty yards in was an opening with a fifteen-foot ceiling. I was below sea level, I thought. The air was wet and fishy. I thought of my childhood trips to the coast where I roamed the shoreline and smelled the barnacles and urchins rotting in the summer heat. It was the smell of the sea. Fishermen cut bait on the piers and left fish parts for the gulls to carry away. All that was left when the pier-fishers went home for the night was the stench of death.

I journeyed further into the subterranean cavern. I didn't see an opening to the sea where marine animals entered the cave to die.

It was quiet and peaceful in the cool, damp darkness. I couldn't hear the ocean or the waves, only the echo of droplets that seeped through the rocks and fell into puddles at my feet.

I looked for evidence that anyone had been here. What would they leave behind, candle wax, rusted flashlights or tools? There was nothing. Someone mortared the ladder into the granite beneath the capstone, but they left no other signs. Maybe workers came here to pillar the foundation when the lighthouse was built, then sealed the

45

opening and walked away. Masons who built the tower must have known about the tunnel.

I decided to come back after dinner with a better light source to explore the walls more closely. Maybe someone left graffiti, or something in the crevices. There was work to do outside. No time now to explore further.

It was a busy day of cleaning everything and checking the equipment, but after dinner, I returned to the well beneath the tower. I shined the light into the opening and saw water. The tunnel was obviously linked to the ocean and water flowed into the cave at high tide. I wondered how far below the floor was the high water line. I'd wait until morning to explore the hidden room I found earlier in the day. A rising tide inside the tunnel would be dangerous, deadly. Perhaps a bioluminescent organism, like plankton, was the source of the mysterious light. It could wash in with the tide and glow when it was agitated in a storm. That made sense.

I wanted to be certain, however. My discovery was part of the island, my island. The room below the tower needed to be explored further.

Chapter 8

The Cavern

By mid-afternoon the following day, I'd laid an electrical cable through the steel door and into the cave. Two halogen lamps illuminated every corner of the subterranean room. I searched the walls for signs of human presence. I was confident that no one had been in the tunnel for a long time. There was evidence that the water rose as much as eight feet at high tide, and flooded the cavern.

I found the source of the seawater on the west wall of the large room. An opening was submerged in a shallow pool. I reached in, but I'd be swimming if I went further. So, I returned to the house, put on a wetsuit, grabbed a scuba mask, and returned to the cave. I stepped into the pool with flashlight in hand, and put my face under water. I submerged and moved into the cavity. It was only after I began to swim through this new tunnel that I thought I might get wedged between the rocks and drown. What if the swim was too long for me to hold my breath? What if I became disoriented before I had enough air to return to the tower? Too, I might emerge into the open ocean and die from the force of waves beating me against the rocks.

I swam on. Even with the wetsuit, I felt my muscles cramp in the cold water.

I thought about turning back, but feared I'd never find the courage again to make a second attempt. I felt claustrophobic. It was a perfect storm to trigger a panic attack, but that would kill me, so I continued on, using the walls on either side to pull myself along.

I had reserve air in my lungs when I emerged in darkness. I used my flashlight to scan the room. I felt sand under my feet. I was chest deep in the water. The ceiling was five feet above me. This room could flood quickly in a rising tide.

My eyes adjusted to the weak light and I saw a glow beneath the surface of the water ahead. I dove and slid through this new opening. A short tunnel opened into the largest cave yet. The ceiling was thirty feet high and the floor was a sand dune. Fifty yards ahead, around a corner, I saw sunlight and heard the sound of waves.

The dankness of the cave fluffed away with a cool breeze of fresh sea air. The mouth of the cavern opened onto a sugar-sand beach, thirty yards wide and twenty yards deep. The open ocean lay before me. The cliffs where the tall pines grew were directly above the sandbar where I stood. I couldn't see the top. I was on the southwest side of the island, facing the mainland. This was the hidden corner of the island where boats could not dock. Just as it was on the top of the cliff, there was no way to scale the granite walls

Principal Keeper

from below. I'd have to risk swimming around the island to the small dock below the tower, or return the way I came, through the maze of tunnels.

I sat on the sand and stared at the open ocean. The waves were calm. It was an illusion that the water on this side of the island was angry and inhospitable. A shallow reef took the bite out of the waves that ran up onto the beach. This place was idyllic, serene. It was the most peaceful spot on the entire island.

I considered the effort to get here, but it seemed a small price for the reward of the view. It was quiet, except for the sound of the gulls and the waves. I'd discovered a hidden beach that could be anywhere in the world: Corsica? Hawaii? Tahiti? No one knew I was here, or how to find me. I couldn't imagine a more isolated place on the planet.

The ocean receded and exposed a reef. It was a barrier that kept boats away from this place. I wondered if anyone had ever been here. Had any of the keepers in over a hundred years discovered this secret? Workers who entered the cave to shore up footings may not have explored further.

I'd discovered a lost world, and was the first to stand where I stood. If I could open the passage between the individual caves in the tunnel, then I could visit this place at will, with little effort. It would be something to consider for the future.

It was time to leave when waves lapped over my feet. The tide was coming in. I had to return to the tower before this new world was flooded.

Chapter 9

Daily trips to the cave became routine. I discovered that a lot of debris from the ocean was deposited in the great room on the beach. The prizes included glass Chinese fishing balls, bottles, boat cushions and a wealth of beautiful driftwood. I gathered some of these items in a diver's bag and took them back to the house. They became colorful decorations on the tables and walls. Hazy green glass and chestnut-colored wood added cheeriness to my living quarters.

The first time I swam through the tunnels and discovered the private beach the light I carried bounced off the granite walls and created shadows that moved along with me, as though I were swimming with dolphins. I thought about the eerie experience one afternoon while I sat on the sand and watched the sunset silhouette the village across the bay. It was late. I needed to head back through the tunnels. I rose to leave and heard a noise from within the cave behind me. My first thought was that a creature like a Harbor seal was in a corner of the cavern. Perhaps a cod or shad was trapped in a shallow pool until the tide rose and carried it back into the ocean. I had company, I thought. Maybe a pet was a good idea, a creature that would listen to my ramblings.

I left the sunlight behind and walked into the cave. A gray haze hung from the ceiling. The flashlight beam was diffused and scattered. I heard the waves on the reef behind me, and droplets fell into the pools. The air was unusually cool and blue, and charged. It felt as if someone was there, hiding, and would step out at any moment to confront me. I listened for the sound to come again, but there was nothing.

"Where were ye, lad? Been ringing for an hour." The harbormaster was on the radio when I walked into the cottage and dropped my swim gear inside the door.

I sat at the desk in front of the radio. "I was on my back in the top of the tower … checking power connections. I didn't hear the bell, and when I did, it took a while to get up and down to the house."

"Well, ya got a government coastal cutter coming through about dusk. Doing their usual bay sounding," the radio crackled off again.

"Bay sounding?" I asked.

"Aye. They test the depths around the harbor. Want to make sure sediment isn't building up from rock erosions and such. There's always trash from the shipping traffic, as well." The radio popped. "It's mostly scientific stuff, keeping their records up-to-date on readings from years past."

Principal Keeper

"Any chance of a storm?"

"Aye, that's why I'm calling, mostly. Cutter will pass close to ya tower. They've been cautioned to put in 'afore too late this evening or risk getting caught out to sea by a big squall. At this point, it looks like a major blow."

"I'll keep my eyes open for them," I said, "and get back to you in the morning."

I signed off and began preparations for the storm. It'd be a late night on the tower.

The weather was fair when I stepped outside. Clouds were high and full, but there was darkness on the eastern horizon. A breeze kicked up, but that was common when the sun warmed the earth.

I knew that storms came on quickly. So, I laid out my rain gear, floodlights, and checked the equipment one last time. Then I went to the top of the tower, pulled out the binoculars, and looked for the Navy cutter.

The harbormaster didn't exaggerate when he said the government vessel would come close to the island. I waved at the crew as they churned through the breakers fifty yards out. White caps broke five to six feet high, and gusts were up to thirty-five knots. Meter needles were moving. Signs were there for a large northeaster, maybe the biggest of the season.

The Navy ship moved north, then turned west for the harbor. They knew well that the elements would soon grow ugly and menacing. I saw their conning tower lights when they reached port.

Rain began to fall and wind gusts peaked at fifty-two knots. It was a wonder how rapidly it came.

I lingered on the balcony for another hour after darkness fell. I studied the choppy water for any private craft or an undocumented tanker that had taken a northern route past Greenland. There were no lights. Not even mysterious ones.

Safe in my stone house, I'd wait out the heaviest part of the storm, then return to my lookout. I ate canned stew, sweet bread and wine for supper. I wrote in my journal. The wind began to buffer the windows, and made it difficult to concentrate. I thumbed through the journal and came across the pages where I spilt water and smeared the ink. Perhaps I imagined too much, but the smudge resembled words. I read *SAVE ME* in the inkblot, but it could have been *SWEAT MEAT*. I decided it was silly to think that the smear appeared to be anything but a stain, a blotch that bled through from words written on the page opposite.

The granite walls shuddered. I closed the journal. The wind howled and the rain battered the windows. I closed the wooden shutters.

I sat in the easy chair near the two-way radio, covered myself with a comforter, and fell asleep. I woke an hour later when I heard a sound. I couldn't tell whether it was in my dream, or somewhere in

Principal Keeper

the room. It came again: a rap on the door. The storm was still hammering the island, so I thought driftwood had blown against the door. I rose and went to open it, but stopped short when the rap came again, louder this time. I hesitated before opening it and peering out. There was nothing resting against it, but it might have blown away.

An hour later, I climbed back into my slickers, hat and boots, and returned to the balcony at the top of the tower. There were no unexplainable, eerie lights or sounds for the rest of the evening. I returned to the keeper's house after midnight and went to bed.

It was noon the following day before the wind died and the rain subsided. Under dark skies, I checked the gauges and recorded the weather measurements for the evening past. I cleared debris off the equipment and reset the breakers to avoid any malfunctions. After dinner, I wrote in my journal and listened to music. There wasn't a broad choice of tunes unless I used my computer to access *Pandora,* or played a CD. The broadcast from the Bellwether Bay radio station was in a sixties and seventies. The female DJ had a seductive "come hither" voice. It was like listening to Kathleen Turner. Her name was 'Misty'. *Really!* I thought. *Does Clint Eastwood know that you moved to Bellwether Bay?* The raspy voice was probably her radio persona, and she didn't look anything as I imagined. Thinking of 'Misty' as attractive made listening to her more interesting.

I climbed into bed, pulled a comforter to my chin, and turned out the light. The radio voice came alive. She stared at me, held out

55

her hand and urged me to take it. It's soft and warm, and I pulled her to me.

I fell asleep quickly. My fantasy with the radio DJ gave way to an unpleasant and familiar dream. It's a different place, another time, in a life distant from my island world. Regardless of what scene I dream of my former professional life, whether good or bad, it always ends the same way. There's loud music and bright lights. I'm in a crowded room. Everyone stares. Their faces are sad or angry or confused. I'm ashamed, contrite, and full of guilt. Their eyes chase me into a glass box that resembles the tower mantel. The glass box rises, and I'm catapulted into space.

Chapter 10

The Blue Lady

The following day dawned gray and wet. I wasn't surprised when the call came in from the weather station. I now possessed the ability to predict both the arrival and relative severity of a storm front. I read the signs, and felt the air and wind on my skin. My senses were heightened and more intuitive to what was coming over the horizon.

When the rain started, I checked the gauges and warning equipment, replaced a fuse in the electrical panel that powered the great horn, and then went to my post on the balcony. I used binoculars to count and record the ships scheduled to pass through into the harbor.

Storms were too frequent this time of year to stop the ships from coming. Lives and industry depended on the movement of the floating monoliths. The fishing season was over, but the great boats continued to plow the North Sea throughout the year, fair weather or foul. Tonight would be rough going for several of these master ships.

The last vessel was so late I had to map its movement in the darkness by the glow of amber bow and conning lights, but it, too, passed safely into dock.

The tide was high and waves broke against the tower's foundation when I headed to the cottage for a late dinner. When I reached the bottom of the stairs, I shined my light into the cave. The water was as high as I'd ever seen. I was staring down into a full well. I reset the stone cap over the opening. If water reached the top, it might seep between the flagstone and concrete, but it wouldn't flood the room.

The tempest continued throughout the night and into the morning. A call to the weather station confirmed that the front had worsened.

"It's not likely to get better for the next thirty hours," the harbormaster reported.

"Any ships coming through?" I asked.

"We caught the rest and routed them south until things quiet down, so you don't need to worry about that, boy." The voice crackled when a percussion of thunder rattled the roof and walls.

"Let me know when you see some relief on your radar," I said.

"We'll do. Keep yer'self dry, now," the voice warned.

The storm grew stronger throughout the evening and into the third day. Sleep was impossible. When I did doze off, my dreams were about life before I came to the island. I was forced to relive the pain I caused others, and the anguish I felt about what I'd done in that former life. Old wounds were opened in these nightmares.

Deep into the fourth night, with the wind and rain battering my stone fortress, I heard another rap against the door. I rose from the bed and went to the landing at the top of the stairs. Debris had once again blown ashore and wedged against the entry, I thought.

The sound came again, then a third time. There wouldn't be any sleep if I didn't dislodge whatever it was from the entry. I went down the stairs to the door. Rain and sea spray rushed in when I opened it. Lightning flooded the room. Then the silhouette of a woman came toward me and I stepped backward into the room. Every corner was saturated in a blue haze, the same light I'd seen from the tower, and through the stones in the floor. This spectral woman was the source.

I saw through her to the storm outside. Her calm, peaceful expression contrasted with the elements that raged behind her. Her hair flew about her neck and face, and her dress pulled at her form. She came closer and I stumbled over the furniture. She turned then, and began to explore the room. I was sprawled on the chair, and watched her float away. She went to the bookshelves, picked up an object and turned to face me. It was a treasure I'd found in the cave, a glass-fishing ball. She held it out, offering it to me.

I wasn't frightened. She wasn't menacing, but her presence was shocking. I was in awe, and wondered if I was dreaming, or experiencing something supernatural.

She was beautiful. Her gown was blue-lace, tattered, and designed for another era. She traveled the length of the room in an instant and was now inches from my face. I caught my breath. She searched my eyes. Then she drifted toward the open door.

"Wait!" I said.

She stopped, turned toward me with a bewildered expression, as though I'd failed to understand her thoughts, and then she began to cry. The sound grew into a wail before she passed out of the room and disappeared in the darkness. I rose from the chair and rushed to the door in time to see a blue hue melt into the tower, and then it was gone.

I felt my heartbeat and saw my breath in the cold air. "Was it real?" I whispered. I rubbed my eyes. I closed the door and started up the stairs. Did my prolonged isolation on the island cause me to hallucinate? Was my mind playing tricks? There were a handful of explanations, none of which involved the supernatural, poltergeists or specters.

I could see her face so clearly in my mind. Who was she, and from where had she come?

Chapter 11

I lay awake before dawn and thought about my discoveries in the caves. Perhaps there were dangerous gasses in the cavern that clouded my mind with dreams of beautiful maidens. Similar to when seafarers reported seeing mermaids. Maybe the isolation was getting to me. I could be lonelier than I thought and craved human contact, and that, then, caused me to hallucinate. Talking to myself was troubling, but seeing ghostly apparitions in the dead of night was a disturbing development.

"Mustn't lose your mind on the job," I said to myself.

I began chores an hour later. Instruments needed checking. There was cleaning to be done. I also wanted to see how my subterranean world was impacted by the storm.

I waited until the sun set and there was only an hour of daylight left before I went below. I made my way through the tunnel and came to the mouth of the cave that opened to the sea. The color of the sky and water told me it would be a peaceful night, unless the spectral dreams came back for another visit.

Frank Pickard

As I turned to leave, something caught my eye. A shiny object was propped on a ledge ten feet above the sandy floor of the cave. I climbed up for a better look, and then fell backwards onto the sand. I hadn't touched it, but I knew what it was. I climbed back up, took it in the palm of my hand, and climbed back down. I spun around, expecting that someone was watching. Then I looked down at the glass orb. It was the same one that the blue lady took from the shelf.

I spent the rest of the evening thinking about her. That the glass ball made its way back into the cavern confirmed she was real. Real? That was absurd. She wasn't real. But it hadn't been a dream either. Someone or something inhabited the island with me. It was a romantic notion with no logic. If ghosts exist, I thought, and a ghost of a young woman was haunting me, then the question was why? Why was she here at Seward? There had to be a record somewhere that would provide clues to the mystery.

I called the harbormaster when I returned to the house.

" Morgan, are you there?" I asked into the radio.

"You still in one piece, Daniel?" he answered.

"Yeah, everything's fine here. A bit of cleanup to do, is all." There was more to do after the four-day storm, but everything was fine for the time being.

"What can I do for you this mornin'?" Morgan asked.

I was grateful to get to the purpose of my call. "Did I read, in a brochure perhaps, that Bellwether Bay has a museum?"

Principal Keeper

"You bet, good one too. Lots of artifacts, photographs and other junk to look at."

"How's the weather look to hold for the next twenty-four hours?" I asked.

"Looks good for a while, particularly after that blow. Why? Do you want a break and come ashore for a visit?" Morgan asked. "Ya been out there alone for a while now."

"You got the idea," I said. "Any chance that can happen?"

"I'll check with the district manager and get back to you, but I don't think they'll have a problem with you getting off the island and having a brief visit here. Might not get this opportunity 'til after the holidays, if you know what I mean."

"Thanks, Morgan. Call me back later."

"You got it, Daniel." The radio crackled and then went silent.

The harbormaster called back, and two hours later I was on the launch. I planned to visit the museum, talk with long-time residents in the village, and gather information on the early history of the lighthouse. The style of the dress worn by the ghost led me to believe she'd lived at the end of the eighteenth, or early nineteenth century.

My possessive feelings about the island extended to the lady. I thought of her as part of my personal, private world, and not to be shared. Besides, it was best I didn't tell anyone I saw ghosts. She was part of the island, the cave, and the tower. These were the things

63

of my world. I wanted to know who she was, how she came to the lighthouse, and why she was there.

It was time to do some research.

Chapter 12

Bellwether Bay

The main thoroughfare in Bellwether Bay fronted the harbor and was lined with tourist shops and restaurants. The museum was a three-storied picturesque Victorian home with gingerbread lace and wrap-around porch. A founder of the community built the home. Captain Jeremiah Woods was a seafaring officer who spent his later years as commodore emeritus of the local yacht club. A painting of Woods in uniform and naval regalia hung in the entry hallway. He held a compass in one hand and a Bible in the other. Tools of the fishing and whaling history of the village adorned the wall behind him as he stared sternly at all who passed into his home.

The museum curator occupied a turret room on the third floor, facing the sea. The rest of the home was dedicated to documenting the history of Bellwether Bay.

The artifacts in the museum, like the items in the commodore's portrait, included ancient tools of the fishing trade that flourished along the coastline since the time of the Vikings. There were carved whalebone, grappling hooks, forged iron riggings, and items chronicling the presence of Nordic explorers.

There was an extensive collection of sepia toned photographs that depicted the founding families, and the lobster fishermen engaged in their trade and the vessels that visited the port. These were the multi-mast wooden and iron brigantines that plied the harbor waters in decades past. There were dozens of photographs and paintings of my historic lighthouse. Polished wooden floors led into rooms furnished just as they were when the original inhabitants occupied the home.

I admired the architectural craftsmanship in the home. My father was a carpenter, so I recognized well-made windows, doorjambs, wainscot, and cornice work. It reminded me of homes in upstate New York, including my own in White Plains.

I was examining tintypes and hand-painted photographs when her voice startled me. "Can I help you find anything in particular?"

She was attractive. Her hair was pulled into a bun. There was gray at her temples. She wore an ankle-length print dress. Maybe it was the uniform of a member of the local art's league or historical society. Her smile was warm and genuine.

"Just looking at everything. Thanks," I told her.

"Tourist?" she asked.

"No, I live here."

Principal Keeper

"Really, then you must be new. I know most everyone who lives here," she said.

"I'm the PK at the harbor light," I said. Historically, principal keepers of the light were respected in the village. Families in Bellwether Bay relied on the light. I had the one position in town that affected the wellbeing of everyone else. "This is my first visit to the village," I told her.

"Ah, yes. I heard a young keeper was on the rock. Welcome to Bellwether Bay."

"Thank you. I went straight out to the island and started my duties a few months ago. This is my first chance to explore the town." I wanted to flatter her. "I thought your museum would be a good starting point."

She smiled. "It is," she said. She glanced around the room, then back at me.

We stared at each other. I turned away and motioned to the wall "Are these the early families, the original settlers?" I asked.

"Yes." She pointed at each one. "These are the Maybells, the Porters, the Puigs and MacClarins. Here are the Kinsingtons and Montgomerys."

"What can you tell me about my new home at Seward Lighthouse?" I asked.

"Oh, I would have thought that Mr. Hobbs, the captain on your shuttle, might have told you everything about the island," she said. "He's traveled back and forth to Seward Lighthouse for decades and knows it better than anyone."

"I don't think Mr. Hobbs likes me. He doesn't talk on our trips or when he brings supplies," I grinned.

"Well, I wouldn't be offended, Mr. ..."

"... Daniel, please," I said.

We shook hands. "I'm Annabelle, or Annie," she said. "People here believe that prolonged solitude and living in the shadow of the tower light can be detrimental to your health. I hope you don't become a barnacled and crusty hermit, Daniel." There was that warm smile again. "There's a whole room on the second floor devoted to the history of the Seward Lighthouse. Follow me."

The walls of the room above were covered with images of the tower: paintings, photographs, many with groups of people in the foreground. They wore wide brimmed hats and bustled dresses. Boys wore knickers and caps, and girls had enormous bows in their hair. You could date the photographs by the clothes.

Annie walked away. She pointed to a spot beside the door. "These pictures here," she said, "are the earliest. They're displayed in chronological order as you move around the room. It's a good, complete photographic history of our harbor light."

There were hundreds of artifacts, including diaries, logbooks and correspondence. The lighthouse was dedicated in May of 1864. The governors of New Hampshire, Rhode Island and Vermont were pictured cutting the ribbon on the stone dock below the tower. A

Principal Keeper

newspaper clipping wrote that Abe Lincoln, the great emancipator, was scheduled to attend the ceremony, but he was busy fighting a war. The tower walls were originally painted red, perhaps for the same reason that schoolhouses of that day were painted the same color. It was cheap. In later years it was striped in black and white paint before it was painted the current white with forest green trim.

Two keepers, a principal and an assistant, were originally assigned duty on the rock. There were more chores without electricity. The warning apparatus, for example, operated manually. A pendulum revolved the light. It worked similar to a cuckoo clock. Weights were raised in the center of the tower and, as they dropped, pulleys rotated the kerosene lamp. From correspondence and journals in the museum, I learned that one of the caretakers kept watch through the night to insure the clock kept turning. Underwater cables were laid in 1931 to bring electricity to the island.

In the early years, keepers were required to be bachelors, because there was a single dwelling to share. In the mid-to-late thirties, a single keeper had the watch and he was permitted to have a wife stay with him. Few photographs showed children on the island, or if they did, the children were generally pre-school age. Children did visit the rock and its majestic tower, however.

I didn't find answers to the questions that brought me to Bellwether Bay. Details were sketchy on the early inhabitants of the island. The blue lady was dressed in a time period close to the turn of the last century. There was a gap in time in the photographs from

69

1932 to 1938. There didn't appear to be any record in the museum of the keepers for those years.

"Finding what you're looking for?" Annie had left the room, and I didn't see her return. I jumped. "I didn't mean to startle you."

"That's fine." I looked down at the table. "I was focused on these log books. I'm not looking for anything in particular," I lied.

"Yes, you are. Even the more serious researchers don't spend as much time in this room as you have today," she told me.

I tried to change the subject. "Do you get serious researchers here?"

"A few," she said. "What is it you want to know?" She smiled.

"Oh, my interest is personal, in as much as I'm the keeper now. I want to know more about the history of my home."

"I understand." She stepped up next to me. "The lighthouse has a distinguished history. But, you don't strike me as a typical keeper."

"Really? How does a typical, seasoned keeper behave?" I asked, and picked up a ledger and thumbed the pages. I hadn't imagined that keepers had a distinct demeanor.

"They're typically hard men," she said, "with salt in their voices, lines on their faces, leather skinned with damaged hands."

"Damaged hands?" I said and looked at my palms.

She took one of my hands. "Damaged hands, callused, broken fingers and missing a nail or two. Not to mention the scars."

70

She ran her fingers over the back of my hand and turned it over. "This is the hand of a stock broker."

I was shocked. I took a step backwards.

"I didn't mean to offend," she said.

I stepped forward as quickly as I'd retreated. "You haven't. Your observations are uncannily accurate. You surprised me."

She took my hand again. "These hands have not been in the lighthouse business for very long."

I liked her touch. It was warm and gentle. I didn't think she was flirting, but her gesture reassured and comforted me. I wanted to take her in my arms and hold her, and tell her how much I enjoyed her kindness. I wanted to somehow, without speaking, say that I appreciated her wisdom and that her touch had reached into my heart.

She seemed to read my thoughts and sensed my insecurities. Annie turned and began to walk away.

"There is one question," I blurted.

She turned.

"There's a gap of time in the books," I said. "I can't find any information about the keepers from 1932 to '38. Was the light not operational during that time? Perhaps it was under renovation."

"With the exception of malfunctions, the light has burned continuously since it opened." She walked to a narrow bookshelf in the far corner of the room. "Here, let's check the harbormaster's logbooks for those years." She turned the pages one-by-one, slowly.

It was my nature to flip through books like they were travel brochures: a habit I acquired scanning financial spreadsheets and stock market reports.

"Here we go, 1928," she read. "Colin Cheswick was the keeper that year. He was the keeper until at least1932, but there isn't any information about when exactly he gave up the post." She picked up the book and carried it across the room and sat in a Windsor chair next to the window. "It says here that he had a family, a wife at least. No kids."

"Does it say how old they were?" I asked.

She sat back. "No, but it's unlikely they were young," she said.

"Why do you say that?"

"Young folk who married in the 1930's usually started a family right away. Their time of service in a lighthouse could be brief if they had a child. Life on a rock was too isolated for children, and dangerous for pregnancies. Minor complications could kill the mother. They might have had babies, but that limited their career.

"Perhaps they never had children," I said. "Or their children were grown."

She closed the book and rested it in her lap. "A lighthouse post on a remote rock was a veteran's assignment. It had to be someone with years of experience. That was the rule in those days. Obviously things have changed." She smiled.

"So no Cheswick kids on the island."

Principal Keeper

"No children, it seems. Nothing about them in this journal." She patted the book.

So the mystery remained. I was no closer to finding clues to the appearance of the blue lady.

I thanked Annie for her time. I glanced back at the house when I reached the gate at the end of the walk. She stood leaning against a porch post, watching me. A breeze rustled the hem of her dress. She pulled a lace shawl over her shoulders. I waved. She hesitated momentarily before waving back. Maybe she had more to tell me. Or maybe she understood that I hadn't shared everything with her.

Chapter 13

Silas MacClarin

I found a sidewalk café halfway up the hill on Main Street, not far from the museum. In front of the 'Chowder Box' was a sign that read, "Fine Food and Great Conversation". Chairs were leaned against the sidewalk tables. The weather was still too cool for open-air dining.

Inside, only two other tables were occupied. I sat in a booth next to the window, facing the street. The sunlight was warm. It was cozy and comfortable. I'd yet to explore Bellwether Bay, but I liked what I saw. I ordered a scallop and grilled salmon entrée with fresh vegetables. The food was great and it reminded me of how poor my diet was on the island. It was the best meal I'd had since I moved to the rock.

I was on my last glass of a half-carafe of wine, and content to watch the sunlight reflect off the whitecaps in the harbor. There was a row of shotgun houses along the street, 1940's vintage. It was choice property fifty yards from the harbor. I saw a figure seated in a deck chair on his porch, motionless, staring at the Bay.

"That's Silas MacClarin. His family was one of the first in Bellwether Bay." The waitress stood over my shoulder. "Crazy fellow, he is."

"Does he come here for meals?" I asked without looking up at her.

"A'ya, he does. Takes meals with us every Tuesday, Friday and most Sundays. He spins tales for the tourists. Lots of larky about his seafarin' grandfather, Angus, and how his father died in the storm of ninety-six and left his mother widowed with twenty babies, or some such." She placed the bill on the table and turned to leave. "He's crazy, sure enough."

I checked the time. I had to be at the dock by six for the trip home. It was one thirty. I walked the street, and stared in the shop windows. Art galleries were a favorite. They had paintings of ships, and images of my lighthouse in fair, and foul, weather. I liked the carvings of whaleboats and schooners. Some places were closed for the off-season. I walked into a bar for a local microbrew before heading back to the harbor.

It was a pleasant day, but I was no closer to solving the mystery of the beautiful and haunting spirit. As I walked down the street toward the bay, I came to the home of Silas MacClarin, who was still seated in the Adirondack chair, staring out toward the harbor and the open sea. I studied the man. Wisps of cob-pipe smoke twirled around his head and shoulders. He looked like an archeological artifact with sun-dried skin and bushy white eyebrows. His eyes were piercing, sea green, and he wore tattered bell pants, a wool pea coat and stocking cap.

Silas' head ratcheted around to look at me.

"Hello," I called, but he didn't respond. I looked down the road. When I turned back, Silas was still staring at me. "Just passing by, headed to the dock." There was no response. "You're Silas MacClarin, aren't you? I heard that you're a local celebrity. One corner of his mouth rose in what I took to be a smile, as good as he could muster. His eyes softened, and he turned back toward the harbor.

"Have you lived here a long time, Mr. MacClarin?" I asked. I had time, and my mission for coming ashore was still unresolved. "I wonder if you could tell me about the history of Bellwether Bay? I was up the hill to the museum earlier. Had a nice chat with the curator, Annie. She has one whole room dedicated to the history of the lighthouse."

I think I struck a cord in old Silas. He grunted, removed his pipe from his lips and spat on the ground beneath the wooden porch.

His voice was stronger than I'd anticipated. "My grandfather was one of the first," he said. It sounded as though he was beginning a litany he'd repeated dozens of times to tourists.

"Yes," I said. "I heard that at lunch today. We frequent the same restaurant." It was my vain attempt to establish rapport with the crusty sailor.

"They was all seamen in my family. Som'a them were born on the water." There was a hint of Irish brogue in his voice and a lot of New England drawl. "Me? I was born on my grandfather's schooner in the middle of a great north'n blow. Aye ya, waves 'ere a breakin' all the way up to the crow's nest. We war'a pitchin' and rockin' in the swells. My mum was down b'low in a hammock swing. That were my first cradle, it was." He stopped and shifted in his seat. "That were the best damn cradle a newborn babe could'a had, she was. They say I went straight to sleep, pitchin', rockin' and all. Born to the sea, they said, in his blood sure, my father told my mum, but she war' gone. Had me, then she gave up the ghost. Hard woman, harder birth, I reck'n."

"I'm sorry, Mr. MacClarin. That must have been difficult, not having a mother to raise you."

"Nah, the sea wer' my mother." His laugh was full of gravel and a barking cough. "She rocked me t'sleep at night, weaned me, gave me a livin' and strengthened me. I had all I er' needed or wanted out there," he said, and motioned toward the water. "I knew her and all of her maids better than any child could'a know'd their own mum and siblings."

I wanted to get to the point of our conversation. "Perhaps you have stories about the harbor light."

"Nobody wants to hear my stories, what I seen, what I know," he groused.

I was certain he was baiting me, imploring me to ask him for more information.

"I do, Mr. MacClarin." I moved closer to the porch.

"Nobody believes me anyway," he said and stared at me. "They all think old Silas is a fruit nut, just plumb full of piss and vinegar. Piss and vinegar," he repeated, as if he were bragging about his local notoriety. He'd often heard the phrase. "They don't want to know the truth, is all."

"The truth?" I asked. "What is the truth, Mr. MacClarin?"

I began to think I'd heard the last from Silas. The sage seemed content to silently stare out at the open water. The wind picked up, and the waves crested five feet high. It was easy to see the white caps from this distance.

Silas closed his eyes and raised his chin to the late afternoon sunlight.

His words were measured this time, as though his lecture to the tourists was over and he was talking to himself. "The truth scares people 'cawz it can be cold and dark, ya' know? It sum'times cuts to yer soul and steals yer wind. It haunts yer dreams and chokes the life out'a yer heart in a steel grip," he said and raised his fist for emphasis. "Ya chase after the truth, think' ya can find peace, but the truth sum'times brings even greater pain. Don't that a'worry ya none, young fella?"

Principal Keeper

"Perhaps, Mr. MacClarin, but sometimes there's no peace without truth," I told him.

"Aye, yer right 'bout that now," he said.

It was time to go to the core of my interest. "What do you know about the history of the harbor light?" I asked. "Have you known the keepers over the years."

"I know'd most of 'em, and my father know'd ones b'fore me," he said proudly.

"What about the keeper in 1928? Did you know that one?"

"That'er the first year they had a single keeper." He savored the pleasure of his intimate knowledge of the details. "The PK were a tall fella' in twenty-eight, long chin, lots of wild hair. He always wore a stockin' cap and pea coat. He chawed a bit, too, like me."

"Chawed?"

"Chewed the cud, tar tabacca, made him spit on the ground a fair bit, it did. His aim weren't too good neither, as I reckleck." He coughed, as if long ago he'd lost the joy in his own humor. He didn't have the strength and breath for a hearty laugh. "Quiet fella'. Kept most to hisself."

He shuffled in the expanse of his chair. I thought he was adjusting his position, moving to release the pain of ancient bones, but Silas labored to stand and put a hand on the porch rail. He paused to settle into his stance and focus on a different perspective of the world. He began to shuffle away.

I called after him. "Did he have family, Mr. MacClarin? The PK in 1928?"

Silas didn't risk disrupting his forward motion to turn and face me. "Wha' say, did who have family?" he asked.

"The PK, in twenty-eight? Maybe a wife, perhaps children?"

"Nah, no family," he said and was gone.

I was disappointed. I had nothing. "Thank you for your time, Mr. MacClarin," I called out, and then turned and continued my trek to the dock.

Chapter 14

I sat at the end of the pier and waited for my ride. I squinted and saw a thousand tiny rainbows dancing in the waves. I thought about the museum and Annie. It'd been a good day, a great salmon lunch, and the weather held fair. But I was no closer to finding the reason for the existence of the blue lady.

There was enough daylight left when I returned home to check the gauges and make a quick trip down into the caves. Shadows were long and thin in the waning light when I reached the great cavern that opened to the water. It was unsettling to think that I might encounter the vision here. She must have known about this place, because I found the glass ball she'd taken from my home.

Lunch earlier in the day was substantial, so I had a light dinner and assumed my vigil on the tower catwalk. The air was cool. A misty rainfall, like sleet, hit my face and hands. Snow and ice were expected in the weeks ahead. I bought a wool stocking cap in Bellwether Bay. It'd be handy when lower temps settled over the island.

I watched three tankers pass the harbor mouth, one after the other. Smaller craft struggled in the surf and wind, but the monoliths hardly flinched in the harsher elements.

I retired to the house at eleven. Before turning out the lights, I received a call from the harbormaster.

"Hope I didn't get you out of bed, Daniel," the voice crackled.

"What' up, got a storm coming through?" I asked.

"Nah, weather looks to hold for another thirty hours or more. That's according to the weather station folks. We're in the calm before the storm. "Kind'a works like that this time of year, ya know?"

I didn't know. Not really. But I was learning. "Yeah, thought that myself," I lied.

"I was radioing to tell you that we got a call from Silas MacClarin this evening. Said he wanted to give you a message. How'd ya meet ol' Silas?" the voice asked.

"We talked when I was in town this afternoon. What's the message?"

"Said to tell you … let me get this straight … here we go. I'll read it to you. Said 'the fella' in twenty-nine married a woman with a kid.'" The radio crackled off.

I waited for more of the message, but the radio went silent. "Was there more to the message, Mr. Cox?" I asked.

82

Principal Keeper

"That was it. He said 'the fella' in twenty-nine married a woman with a kid,'" he repeated. "Whatever that means. Does it make sense to you?"

"Yeah, I think I know what he means. Say, any chance I could get a couple more hours in town tomorrow? I didn't finish the shopping I planned, and I'd like to taste that salmon at the 'Chowder Box' one more time before I get stuck out here for a while."

"I can arrange that. Sure. But I suggest you try the seafood bisque at the 'Rusty Pelican' this time." The radio popped, then the voice said, "Toby'll be there early, just after sunrise, to run you in."

"I'll keep an eye out for him," I promised and signed off.

✳✳✳

I went straight to Silas' when I reached the mainland the next morning. Sleet was coming down and the wind-chill was forty-five degrees.

I pulled my collar up and approached his porch. The chair was empty, the house was dark and no one answered when I knocked. I looked at the chair. It'd been painted a dozen shades of green, much of which had chipped away. It resembled a patchwork quilt. The armrests were worn to bare wood. I sat in it. What a wonderful view the old man had here on his porch. I'd be content in my senior years with a restful spot similar to this each morning and evening.

I had until after lunch before I had to be back on the dock. Weather reports predicted a front coming through in the evening hours. I had to be on the island by two to make preparations. I'd enjoy lunch and drop back by Silas's before heading to the harbor.

Most of the main-street shops were closed as I walked up the hill. Tourist trade was nearly nonexistent this time of year, and shop owners who lived further inland closed early to get home before dark. If the weather soured before they left, they could get trapped in their stores.

I came to the 'Rusty Pelican', but decided to walk a block further to where I knew the food was good. I was early, but I skipped breakfast to meet the launch, so I was hungry. With the cold outside, a warm bowl of chowder and a smoked salmon entrée were calling out to me.

The waitress recognized me from the day before. She took my order, but this time she encouraged me to try the lobster on my next visit.

It was twelve forty when I went to the register to pay the check. I had time to stop by Silas' home again.

"Did ya git the message I sent!" It was Silas. He'd just come through the door.

I turned to face him. "I did. Thank you." I motioned to a booth in the corner. "Can I buy you a cup of coffee, Mr. MacClarin?" I asked.

Principal Keeper

Silas scooted across the room as I ordered the coffee and brought it to the table.

"Mind if I have a slice of peach cobbler?" Silas asked.

It was the first time I saw him grin. It resembled the fence in his front yard with most of the pickets missing.

I laughed. "Not at all," I said and ordered.

He held the hot cup in the palm of his hands. The bones in his fingers resembled twigs covered in wet cheesecloth. Blue spider veins covered the back of his hands.

Neither of us spoke until he finished his pie. He used his fingertip to mop up the peach filling on the plate. Then he sat back, wiped his chin and lips with the napkin, and looked at me for the first time.

"The PK in twenty-nine was married," he began. "Colin Cheswick was his name."

"How do you remember his name?" I asked.

"Hard to forget that one, what with all the trouble he had."

"What kind of trouble, Mr. MacClarin?" I asked.

"Don't know for sure. When they found the child, she was wilder than a sea otter in a lobster trap."

"They had children?" I said.

"Aye, one, I think." Silas turned to look out the window.

"How old was the child?" I asked.

"Maybe six, maybe twelve. Not certain. She was wee is what I remember."

85

"Tell me about Cheswick, Mr. MacClarin."

"He was a gloomy fello', alwas' had a frown on his face. 'Course he weren't no young beaver neither. Maybe fifty-five, sixty when he first came to Bellwether Bay."

"You say he was probably sixty, but he had a six year old daughter?"

"Aye, but weren't his pup, you see. It was her's."

There was that sly, gappy-toothed smile. Silas was enjoying the clever way he revealed the information.

"Everyone talked about how much older he was than his wife. Lady Cheswick was dainty, young, with long hair and green eyes," Silas told me. "Ever'one wondered about that pair. Him so much older than she were, you know? Some said she had to be a floozy, that wha' say the old biddies in the village, and some said the old man got lucky to marry hisself a purty lass like that."

"Do you remember her name?" I asked.

"Don't recall. I barely remember his," Silas said.

"What's the trouble Cheswick had that you mentioned a moment ago?"

"Well, it's only a guess, mind you, but I think he murdered that young wife of his and then he couldn't live with what he done." He looked out the window again, as though he longed for his porch chair and view of the bay.

"What happened to the Cheswick's?"

Principal Keeper

"Agin, it's only speculation, but some say he kilt her then took his own life."

"Cheswick committed suicide?" I said, shocked.

"That 'ere the way it looked, yeah." Silas paused for dramatic affect before his next remark. "And they n'er found his wife's body. Never. Some thought he threw her into the ocean and that she'd eventually wash ashore, but she never did," Silas said.

"And the baby, what happened to the baby, Mr. MacClarin?" I was anxious.

"They say the baby was found sitting on the cold stone floor, smack dab in the middle of the tower, crying and staring up at the dangling corpse of old Colin Chezwick hanging from the rafters. She howled like a banshee when they went to take her away. I hear'd that she grew up in an orphanage somewhere in Jersey, then they say she went to the nut house."

"Cheswick hung himself in the tower?" I asked.

"Seems so. Some said that his beautiful wife took up with a young teacher here in the village and the two of 'em kilt the old man, and run off together, abandoning her baby and all. That were the town biddies talkin' agin."

"Why would she leave her baby behind?" Silas was spilling out a wealth of facts, and I wanted to encourage him to keep talking.

"'Cause that were the only way to convince everyone that she were dead too, like the old man. Least ways that what's the biddies

87

said. No one would believe that a mum would abandon her own child like that, even for sinful love."

"Didn't she know the baby would die alone out there?"

"Now you're asking questions I have no recollection of. How's I to know what she knew or didn't knew? Besides, there was an SOS from the rock that led the harbor authorities to investigate and find his body, and the youngun sittin' on the floor cryin'. So, if she did run off, she knew the baby would be found in time, a'for anything bad happened to it."

He paused again to take a drink from his freshly filled cup. "Me? I think he just up and kilt her 'cause she was so purty and he couldn't stand to think about another man getting' his hands on her. Then he kills hisself after he sobered up an' seen what he done."

"So he drank?" I asked.

"Aye, we all did. Some more'an others, and he, if I recall correct, more than most. He liked Irish rum, I think. I know'd that 'cuz he would pick up a cask when he came to town for provisions. I worked in my uncle's store in those days and I seen Chezwick and the lady come in from time-to-time. She alwa's wore this same pretty dress, green or blue. I remember 'cause it matched her green, purty eyes. And she'd pile that long, wavy hair up on top of her head. Yessir, she was a looker."

Silas sat silent, then. I suspected he was lost in memories of the young woman and his own youth. I used the silence to mentally sort through what I'd learned from Silas' ramblings. He seemed

Principal Keeper

certain of his story, and pleased with the details he'd remembered and shared.

"I best be getting' home. Gotta feed Chester," Silas said as pushed his cup away and rose.

"Who is Chester, Mr. MacClarin?" I asked and helped him up from his seat.

"He's my collie. Scottish Border Collie, he is, best herding dog known to man, smart as the mast is straight. Keeps trying to herd me around the house." He began his shuffle to the door.

I paid the bill and followed him outside, where he was already making his way across the street.

"Thank you, Silas," I shouted after him, not knowing whether he heard me or not.

I stood at the corner and watched to make certain Silas made it safely across the street. He stopped, then, and turned to face me.

"Caroline, her name was Caroline!" he called out.

Chapter 15

The Demon in the Storm

I had history and a name for the blue lady, but questions remained. What became of her, and why was her spirit on the rock?

Waves were choppy when I set foot on the island. Humidity was up. The air was briny. A storm was coming and I had work to do. Preparations were needed before wind, rain and seas raked over my slip of land. Clouds gathered in the east, and a gray-green light painted everything.

The pulse of a seasoned mariner quickened in the peaceful, deceiving calm before a storm. It began with a breath of warm air across my cheek, a whisper that gave way to a gust of cold wind. Within the hour, a demon came ashore and began to beat down from all directions.

When darkness came, curtains of rain fell over the island. The wind blew from all compass points, and made walking a straight line impossible. I was dressed for battle with my boot straps tight, slicker buckled high on my neck, and stocking cap pulled low and

Principal Keeper

dry under my rain hood. The wind howled and screamed as I moved, hand-over-hand, along the guideline to the tower. I paused before I stepped out onto the catwalk. I recalled a time when my father took me fishing and we got caught in an electrical storm. We huddled in sleeping bags in the dryness of our oilcloth tent until my father got up and stepped outside. A flash of lighting silhouetted his figure, arms outstretched, onto the wall of the tent. When he crawled back inside, I asked why he risked being struck by lightning.

"The lightning wasn't going to hit me, son," he said.

"How do you know?" I asked.

"Because it's not my time," he said so decisively that I didn't doubt him.

He turned away, onto his side, and fell asleep. His philosophy was comforting and plausible in a mystical way. Lightning can't hurt you if you're convinced that it isn't your time to die. Fear was the enemy. To believe in your heart that you're safe in the face of death, gave you incredible powers to defy the elements, to risk your life, and to challenge the odds. I stepped out onto the catwalk.

I gripped the railing and turned my shoulder into the gale. The red harbor marker lights were barely visible. Only my powerful candle broke through the tempest.

No ships were expected. There was no reason to be here, but it was my favorite post in these storms. I also wanted to prove that it was not my time, just as my father had done. I felt at peace.

I stepped back into the lamp house, checked the mechanisms, and began the long trip down the spiral stairs. Halfway down I felt the air around me grow colder with each step. I looked over the railing. A green haze illuminated the floor below. Ten steps from the bottom, I walked into an eerie fog. My breath hung in the air. The haze slipped over each step as it came toward me. It enveloped me, then moved on toward the top of the tower. Then I heard the capstone. I'd secured it after my last visit to the caves. From three steps up, I saw that the stone lid was undisturbed, but the sound persisted.

I cupped my hands, blew air into them, and moved toward the door. Something dark and oppressive hid in the mist. Some otherworldly entity stood with me in the stillness of the tower. My heart raced. I felt embraced and suffocated by a sinister force.

I reached the door, swung it wide and was hit by a blinding light. The shock threw me back into the room. I felt hands claw at my legs. I stood and rushed through the door. I reached for the guideline, but it wasn't there. I crawled on hands and knees, reached and opened the door to the cottage, and fell into the middle of the room.

The entity I encountered in the tower was different. It wasn't the blue lady. This new force was evil and threatening. I didn't fear the lady, but I was frightened in the tower. It wasn't what I witnessed, but what I'd felt. The lady meant me no harm, but I was in danger with this new presence.

Principal Keeper

The storm continued throughout the night. A gray, wet dawn waited as I stepped outside. I found nothing in the tower that hinted at my experience. It was raining, but the winds were calm. It was forty-two degrees by mid-morning. I wore a heavy pea coat and stocking cap under my rain gear. The weather front would hold for another day or two, so it didn't make sense to do a cleanup. The foghorn and lamp operated properly. The brassy blare from the horn cut through the fog, and the light scanned the ocean: out then back, out then back.

I retreated to the warmth of my ceramic stove and wrote in my journal. I needed time to think, to consider everything that had no logical explanation. If Colin Cheswick committed suicide in the tower, was it his spirit I met last night? If he murdered Caroline, was he now trying to harm me? Would I have to endure visits from the two, the lady and the ghost of her alcoholic husband for as long as I lived on the island?

Was I losing my mind? Was I hallucinating everything? Some people believed in ghosts, but there wasn't any hard, definitive evidence. Was I ready to become a believer in the paranormal?

I decided that what happened in the tower and on the night Caroline came to visit me in the cottage were real. I wouldn't deny the experiences. I wasn't losing my marbles.

I didn't feel isolated any longer. Two spirits, one sinister, the other innocent and maternal, roamed the grounds. They were

93

chained to this rock, damned to spend eternity in restless, nocturnal stirrings. I would learn to live with it all.

But the picture was incomplete. Colin Cheswick and his young, attractive wife were alone together on the island long ago, and no one knew the whole story about what happened to them. Caroline's disappearance was a mystery. She was never found. And Colin's reason for committing suicide, if that's what he did, was lost to time. Too, what became of their child?

I returned to the tower late in the afternoon and spent an hour monitoring traffic moving in and out of the harbor. I considered lifting the stone and exploring the tunnels, but another storm was predicted in the next six hours and the tide would be high.

I was exhausted, not having slept the night before. I was grateful to lock down the island and get into bed. I visited the foghorn shanty, and then climbed the stairs to check the gauges and warning devices in the tower.

Once in bed, I fell into deep slumber. The storm beat down on the island, but I'd learned to sleep through the din. The drone of the foghorn every thirty seconds was more a comfort than a disruption. It was a heavy blanket, a hollow ode to isolation, my warm companion beneath the covers.

Principal Keeper

Unlike other nights, my dreams were moderately pleasant. It was a beautiful day as I walked up the driveway of our suburban home. My son rushed wildly, recklessly out of the front door to meet me. I picked him up and swung him above my head, and then walked him to the house. Cradled in my arms, I smelled the sweetness in his hair. His mother met us in the entry. Her expression was angry and accusing.

"You have the nerve to come back," she said. "Paul was here. I know about the dirty deals you and Daddy made!" She took our son from my arms. I started to speak, but she interrupted me. "Do you know how many people you've hurt? Did you think about that, Daniel? Did you? I always knew Daddy could be sleazy with his business dealings, but I never expected it from you." She turned away. "You should have thought about the consequences before you ruined my family, your family. You had no regard for the lives you've hurt with your greed and wiping out the life savings of the investors who trusted you." She shouted over her shoulder, "Get out and don't come back!"

I came out of the dream, sat up and leaned against the headboard. The rain was a drizzle now. I heard it patter above the open-beamed ceiling. I pulled the comforter up. I was warm, rested. I waited for the emotion of the dream to slip away. The mistakes and foolishness that broke my family apart didn't matter any longer. Time softens emotional wounds and the scars they leave behind.

95

Chapter 16

I'd dozed off with the blanket under my chin when a bolt of lightning struck the middle of the room near the foot of the bed. I didn't see the flash, but the crescendo split the air so loudly that I jumped to my feet. I now stood on the pillows and braced myself against the wall behind my bed.

The walls melted slowly away like a Salvador Dali painting until I was exposed to the elements. The tower loomed above me. My bed hung precariously on the remnants of the hallway balcony. As I watched, the tower morphed into a colossus. Poseidon rose out of the ocean and leaned toward me. The tower light was his eye. He crouched closer. One hand held a schooner with tattered sails. The name of the boat was 'Lost Souls'. Another flash of lightning and the giant raised the sailboat above his head and hurled it at me. It grew larger as it came closer.

My scream brought me out of the dream. A final rumble of thunder and Poseidon was gone, and the walls of the house were intact. I'm buried in sheets and blankets.

Principal Keeper

"Only a dream," I whispered. "A nightmare." I rose. "Maybe it's all been one giant nightmare." I walked into the bathroom. "Maybe I am losing it. Maybe I can't take the stress of isolation, so my mind is crafting ghosts and sea monsters."

"You need a new attitude, Danny Boy," I said as I dressed, donned rain gear and headed out to my duties. It'd be light in a couple hours, although the sunlight these days was stifled and diffused. But I wanted to get an early start on all of the tasks left in the wake of the storm's rampage.

In the cold dawn, I decided to walk the island and scout for debris. I found pieces of decking and colorful scraps of nylon sail sheeting, and thousands of displaced crabs, sea urchins and shellfish. Sea grass saturated with black tar from the tankers was draped over the rocks along the shoreline.

The day grew brighter, but the sky was filled with smoky clouds full of rain and an occasional burst of lightning. Gusts jostled me as I went about my chores. I'd learned that the wind was a constant out here on the water. I didn't mind.

I raised the stone to check on the condition of the caves. The tunnels beneath the tower were real, even if everything else was a nightmare. I wasn't ready to conclude that I was going mad with all of the strange visions and dreams. I had to be stronger mentally if I were going to remain on the island.

The lid was unusually heavy, as though the edges had settled back into the grout. With the capstone pushed aside, I shined the light into the well. The water at the bottom was high. Otherwise, all looked undisturbed by the storm. A break in the nasty weather was expected in the next twelve hours, so I left the hole partially open to allow for easy access when the tide receded.

Ships and tankers were ghostlike in the misty afternoon air. It was an opportunity to check the seals on the potable storage tanks. There was a constant risk that brine would seep in and contaminate the drinking supply. I also planned to clean the reflectors, and remove salt deposits on the lamp house windows. The tarnished brass surfaces would wait for sunnier days.

After a light meal, I took my post on the tower balcony. I'd stashed a campstool in the mantel house. I sat with my back against the lamp enclosure and propped my feet on the railing. With my spyglass to watch the traffic, I was as comfortable as I could be with rain dripping off my cap, and occasionally into my coffee.

I stayed longer than usual, and logged the passing vessels. It'd been a full day, but I'd had time to refocus on why I'd come to Seward Lighthouse. It was a noble duty to protect the mariners and their families, many of whom lived in the village. It dawned on me that coming out here freed me from the unanswered personal questions in my life. I was torn emotionally when I took this job. Leaving my son behind was the most difficult part of it all, but his mother wasn't going to let me get too close to him anyway.

Poor weather was a nuisance, at first, but in time I welcomed the challenge. I convinced myself that I'd sleep well tonight:

Principal Keeper

certainly better than I had the previous evening. I found peace and purpose in my surroundings. I'd left chaos behind in New York, and discovered a rewarding life in this solitary place.

There were no strange lights or fogs when I descended the tower stairs. No need for the guide-wire when I made my way back to the house. I read for a while, checked in with the harbormaster as required, and then wrote a few pages in my journal. I went to bed early.

I stirred only once, to go to the bathroom and get a drink of water. I woke in the early morning hours before dawn. A blue light bled through my eyelids. I kept them shut. I knew that the lady was there in the room. Her presence was brief, but profound. Near the end of her visit, the light on my eyelids grew more intense. She was close. It was then that I felt her spirit blanket me. I felt her pain and sorrow. I felt her extreme loneliness. The blue light faded and darkness came again. Outside, beyond the walls of the house, I heard her wail, and then she was gone.

Chapter 17

New Responsibilities

The day came gray and drizzly. The lady's visit weighed on my mind. I wanted to know more. I was certain that an extraordinary event held her captive on the island and in the caverns beneath the tower. I'd felt her sadness, her loneliness and torment. More than ever now I wanted to unlock her secret. She carried a weight in her afterlife, and I'd been tasked with unraveling the mystery of the chains that bound her to this place. I feared that if I didn't pull her into the light, she might drag me into the shadows.

The lady was never far from my thoughts as the days passed and I went about my business at the Seward Lighthouse. Perhaps I was meant to come to this place. I could see where the journey to the island began long ago. I was exactly where I was supposed to be at this time in my life. It was inevitable that I'd be the person to unravel the mystery. It became a task as great as the responsibility of the harbor light. Both involved saving lost souls; whether it was an errant ship full of weary seaman, or a ghostly woman in blue.

Principal Keeper

A week came and went, then another, and there was no sign of her. I wondered if I'd ever see her again. My journal became a repository for theories. Mostly, I made a list of questions. Questions like, Was she Caroline Cheswick, wife of the former keeper? If so, then her spirit had been here for a very long time. Also, why hadn't my predecessors mentioned her? Perhaps my discovery of the caves freed Caroline's spirit. I wanted more than anything else to know why Caroline chose me to haunt.

My journaling was prophetic. One evening, my wishes were granted.

The day began pleasant, but by nightfall a storm came and battered the tower and stone house. My talent for sleeping through the assaults was established, but on this night I woke to the sensation of a tug on my coverlet. It was slight, but enough. I turned my head to the side and opened my eyes. A child leaned against my bed with a fist full of my blanket. I watched as they turned and tottered across the room to the open door. I sat upright. The floorboards, doorframe and hallway balcony railing were visible through the child's translucent form. It was Caroline's baby!

I threw back the covers and ran after the child, but when I reached the landing, the apparition was gone. I watched as the front door opened and an adult figure materialized in the doorway. They came forward into the middle of the room. They were dressed in a Navy-blue seaman's coat and wool cap. I couldn't see his feet, or whether he wore boots.

I wanted to run back into the bedroom, lock the door and hide under the blankets. Before I could move, the man's face turned upward. I was frozen by his stare.

"Caroline!" His words echoed through the house. His voice was distant, as though it floated out of a tunnel. "Caroline! Where be ye?" he called out. His expression softened. "Ah, there ya ar."

The spirit of Caroline was by my side, her hands next to mine on the railing. She stared down at the old man. Neither of them seemed to notice me. This was a scene from the past, and our roles were reversed. Now, I was the ghost for these two lost souls. She turned and descended the stairs. When she reached the seaman, they pivoted and walked out into the storm. The door closed and I was alone.

There'd be no more sleep tonight. A new dimension of contact was formed in this latest encounter between the spirits and myself. Never again would I deny or doubt their presence. I wondered when they'd come again.

Caroline looked markedly different than when I'd first seen her. Tonight her hair was pinned up and her dress was not tattered. I'd witnessed a moment in time before her distress, I thought.

In the dark hour before the new day, I concluded that I'd witnessed a burst of psychic energy that left me with more questions. The story was unraveling in bits, but I was no closer to solving the tragedy that entombed the lady and her family.

Chapter 18

Addison Frances Gilbert (McHenry)

I woke seated in the overstuffed chair on the main floor. My eyes fluttered open and I struggled to focus on the room. I felt as though I'd slept for several days. My body ached. My limbs were knotted. It took effort to sit up in the chair. My eyes were dry and my head throbbed.

I made my way to the kitchen and found the aspirin. I leaned on the counter and waited for the medication to ease my discomfort. It was then that I heard a knock on the door. My first thought was that the spirits had returned, but then I remembered they only came at night, in a storm and rarely bothered to announce their arrival. Then I thought the knock was just the pounding in my head, but it came again. I moved to answer it. The light that screamed through the open doorway seared my eyes and added to the pain in my head. Human silhouettes stood in the entry.

"Catch you at a bad time, Mr. Riggs?" the superintendant asked as he and several others stepped through. I moved to the side as the entourage passed. "Not fair, I know, to surprise you like this, but I am required to make occasional unannounced visits. Nothing to worry about, really, and, honestly speaking, this is more of a tour. I have a handful of distinguished guests joining me on this visit.

I attempted in vain to wipe the creases from my shirt, and ran my fingers through my hair. "Long duty last night, Mr. Mason," I said. "Big storm."

"Yes, we know. Weren't certain we'd make it out this morning, but things began to burn away about five AM.

I was annoyed by the casual, invasive manner the superintendant wandered the room, inspecting objects on the shelves and the papers on my desk.

"Mr. Riggs," he said as he walked, "I'd like to introduce Mr. and Mrs. Willard, Mrs. Jessup, and Miss Addison Frances Gilbert."

The young woman named "Addison" stepped forward. "Hello, Mr. Riggs. It's a pleasure to meet the principal keeper of the Bellwether Bay harbor light.

I was embarrassed by the unexpected visitors from the moment I opened the door, but never more so than in that moment. She was beautiful, graceful and charming. Her smile was familiar, warm and captivating. I liked her instantly.

"Thank you, Ms. Gilbert," I said, shaking her hand. "It's my pleasure as well."

The superintendant's voice broke the moment. "Riggs, would you mind showing us the facility? Mr. Willard and his wife are ministry associates who sit on the Board of Examiners for the Canadian government, appointed by the prime minister, you see. And Mrs. Jessup is from our home office in Toronto. She has the unenviable task of reporting the state of our readiness here, as much responsible for the existence of this post, that is to say your job, as anyone here."

"Of course I don't mind showing everyone around the facility." I was still holding Addison's hand. "And you, Ms. Gilbert? Why have you come to visit the rock?"

"Miss Gilbert is a local Bellwether Bay heroine, of sorts," the superintendant said. "She's the daughter of a prominent, local citizen, a distinguished benefactor. Miss Gilbert is home from college. She's in advanced studies at a prestigious school in New York."

"Columbia," she said.

I released her from my grip. "If you will allow me a few minutes to wash my face and change my clothes, I'll be with you shortly and we can have a look about the island." I moved toward the door in an overt gesture that everyone should wait outside.

When I emerged from the house, most of the group had gathered a short distance away. Clustered together, they resembled the colony of gulls that perched on the rocks by the breakers to the south.

Addison, however, stood alone on a ledge, looking out across the water, her hands folded behind, holding a straw hat embellished

105

with a green ribbon. She'd meant for the hat to be cover from the sunlight, I thought, but it was destined never to stay on her head in the wind that forever blew across the island this time of year. The air was still chilly from the previous night, but she was the image of a carefree tourist on summer holiday by the sea. Her dress blew against, and accentuated, her form. She had a delicate figure. I was pleased that she'd come to my island.

It was not until we'd all stepped into the tower that I thought about the flagstone and the caves below. I hesitated until I saw that the lid was closed. All was in its proper place as our group stood in the lower tower room.

Everyone began to ascend the spiral stairs. Addison went first, and climbed so quickly that she left the group behind. Her steps barely made a sound as she took them two at a time, unlike Mrs. Jessup and the lady Willard, who both wore heels that made it difficult to walk up the porous, honeycombed metal steps. The superintendant, Willard and I brought up the rear.

It was an effort to get everyone into the lamp house. Addison had already found the door out onto the catwalk and was strolling around the mantel. Unfortunately, I was occupied with helping to get the others up into the tower and answering questions about the operation of the lamp. But, I kept an eye on Addison's movements.

"Can we join Ms. Gilbert outside, Mr. Riggs?" Mrs. Willard asked.

106

Principal Keeper

"Of course," the superintendant answered before I could speak.

"I'll wait for you here, dear," Mr. Willard said.

"I'll keep you company, Mr. Willard," Mrs. Jessup said. "I've seen my share of tower views in service to the ministry."

I stepped outside and stood next to Addison. "Not afraid of heights, Ms. Gilbert?"

"Not at all. I think it's wonderful up here. You have a marvelous view of the sea and the mainland. I'd love to live on the island. I'd visit this place on the tower each day," she said.

"I spend most of my time on this balcony," I told her. "You should see it at dusk and in the evening. On a clear night," I said, looking upward, "the sky looks as though it were sprinkled with powered sugar. There are so many stars that their light clusters together into a milky cloud."

"Can we move on to see the rest of the operation, Mr. Riggs?" Superintendant Mason asked.

The party made their way back down to the bottom of the tower. Everyone filed through the door except Addison, who stood directly over the stone in the center of the room and stared upward toward the lamp housing.

"You must find incredible peace in your tower, Mr. Riggs," she said.

"I do like it, yes," I said and motioned her toward the door.

107

They inspected the foghorn facility, the weather station equipment where I took regular readings, and then I led them on a walk around the island. We stopped for a bit on the cliffs above the secret cave.

"The water looks unusually angry here on this side of the island, Mr. Riggs," Mrs. Jessup said.

"The reef formations and granite walls, coupled with the wind, do make for rough seas down there," I conceded.

"Have you ever climbed down to the water?" Mr. Willard asked.

"No, I wouldn't want to risk getting swept into the ocean by the waves. Besides, there doesn't appear to be any way down. The walls are too shear," I said.

I thought about the cave opening below us, and the sandbar where I watched the sunsets, and the solitude I experienced in the great cavern.

"Are you certain there's no way to get down, Mr. Riggs?" Addison asked. She leaned and looked over the edge so far that I felt my heart skip.

For a moment, I thought she might know about the existence of the caves, but I was convinced she was only intrigued by the prospect of exploring the island further.

I assumed a profession demeanor. "Even if there were a way down, my business is up here." I looked around. Mason and the Willard's were listening. "I have little free time to idly repel these cliffs," I said. "Too dangerous, as well. No one would ever find me if I fell."

Addison smiled and winked at me. She understood my purpose in making the remark in front of the others.

"Right you are, Riggs," Mason said. "I'm sure that Mrs. Jessup is pleased to hear that you stay focused to your task here on the rock."

We took our time returning to the courtyard in front of the house.

"I wish I had a brunch to serve you all," I said.

"Not necessary," Superintendant Mason announced. "We have plans to dine at the 'Chowder Box.'"

"I won't be joining you, Mr. Mason," Addison said. "Mother is expecting me. She gets so little time with me on these breaks from school. She isn't fond of sharing her only daughter." She approached. "Thank you for the wonderful tour, Mr. Riggs," she said, then shook my hand. "I hope to see you in the village some day. You can't spend every moment enjoying that captivating view from the tower." She looked around. "In fact, I envy you the beauty you have everywhere on your rock, as you call it."

"I hope you'll consider coming back to visit," I told her. The warmth of her touch and her sea-green eyes distracted me. "I hope you'll all consider coming back for a visit," I said to the group. "It gets lonely here sometimes, and visitors are always welcome."

Everyone turned to the sound of the approaching launch.

"Thanks again, Mr. Riggs," Mason said as he walked away. "I'll send out a copy of Mrs. Jessup's report when I receive it."

"It shouldn't take me long to write," Jessup said, and then shook my hand. "You run a tight ship, I must say. Very clean and well maintained. I commend you."

She flattered me. "Thank you, Mrs. Jessup," I said.

I helped everyone to board the launch, and then stepped back on the dock and watched their departure. The boat began its slow, chugging move away from the rocks. I started to turn and head up the hill when a voice called out and I turned.

"Mr. Riggs! I almost forgot. My mother said to say 'hello,'" Addison shouted.

"Your mother?"

"Yes! You met her in the village! Annie Gilbert! She's the curator of the museum, Jeremiah Woods' home." Her words were barely audible above the roar of the engine, but she smiled and waved.

That was enough.

Chapter 19

The scent of gardenias hung in the air of the cottage. I also smelled them in the tower room and mantel housing. Addison Frances Gilbert left behind an impression, as well as a memory.

My step was lighter when I began chores.

I felt certain the visitors hadn't noticed the piles of sea grass and driftwood left behind by the storm. Thank goodness, I thought, that more human-made debris had not washed ashore this time. A ripped and soggy boat cushion against the tower door might have left a negative impression with the inspector and superintendant.

I lifted the stone lid to check on the caverns. There were puddles in the bottom of the shaft, but everything appeared normal. I'd wait for a quieter day to visit the solitude of the secluded beach beneath the cliff. Perhaps someday I'd share my secret world with Addison.

With a cup of tea from my evening meal, and the sunlight bleeding away, I was on my stool on the balcony. Shadows of Addison were everywhere. I was impressed that she went straight to the catwalk the moment she reached the lamp house. I could still see her, distorted by the glass windows, as she moved along the railing. It was most probably there that the wind ripped her straw hat from his grasp and carried it out to sea, because I couldn't remember seeing it again. Her gaze when we shook hands and said 'goodbye' would stay with me for a time.

There was much to consider about Addison's short visit. Would she ever return, I wondered? Would she be visiting her mother when I, once again, broke loose and went ashore?

The most wonderful thing about her trip to Seward, aside from our meeting, was that she'd freed me from the nightmare. Thoughts of Addison, and speculating on when we'd meet again, were a respite from the mystery of the lady.

Chapter 20

Calm weather held steady for several days. I visited the caverns twice, but the tidewater remained high and cold beneath the tower. Dreams were pleasant, no visits from ghostly figures, and no wailing in the night. I read and wrote in my journal, and polished the brass figures on the equipment.

Addison stayed on my mind. Her visit whetted my desire for companionship. I'd considered getting a dog or cat, perhaps a budgie or parakeet. A mutt could negotiate the spiral stairs. There were pictures in the museum of other keepers with their dogs. Maybe it was my time. I decided to find a canine companion when I visited the village after the holidays.

One day a colony of seals visited the far end of the island. They lay on the rocks for several hours under a weak winter sun. I approached, but when I crossed the invisible line of territorial domain, the largest of the gang barked and I backed away. It would be fun, I thought, to have a dog to chase them back into the water.

As the holidays approached, I decorated with starfish and candles. I found two clay butter molds in the kitchen with ornament designs, and I hung them on the mantel. The local radio DJ's voice was warm and sugary as she played holiday classics.

I received a package on Christmas Eve. The water was too rough for the launch to dock, so the boatman came as close as he could and flung the package to me as I stood on the pier.

"Happy Holidays, Mr. Riggs," he shouted and smiled. I'd never seen him smile.

"Thank you, and the same to you," I shouted back.

The box was heavily taped, but the package inside was wrapped in festive holiday paper. Inside were greeting cards, corn muffins, cookies and cakes from the villagers. The 'gang' at the 'Chowder Box' sent a large serving of smoked salmon.

I didn't feel cheated being isolated and alone for Christmas, but the kindness and generosity of their gifts, and the expressions of appreciation in the cards were more than I expected. I felt very much a part of the Bellwether Bay community, and I was moved by the kindness of these strangers.

At the bottom of the box was a legal sized envelope marked "To Mr. Riggs from Addison Gilbert." I moved to the reading chair to open it. Inside was a two-page, hand written letter and a Christmas card. The card had a Currier and Ives scene with glitter for the snow. It was postmarked in New York and addressed to me, and mailed in care of *Annie Gilbert, Bellwether Bay Museum 924 Harbor Blvd., Bellwether Bay.* Inside, she'd written, *Best wishes for the holidays,* and signed it, *Addison.* So, her Christmas wishes to me went through

Principal Keeper

her mother. Addison was obviously comfortable having Annie aware our friendship.

I stood the card upright on the lamp table and turned my attention to the letter.

Addison began by thanking me again for the tour and commenting on how much she'd enjoyed the view from the tower. She explained that she'd lived in Bellwether since she was fifteen, when her mother moved back to the community. Evidently, Annie was born in the village. Addison wrote about how she'd always wanted to visit the lighthouse, but never had the chance when she was growing up. Living in New York, now, and soon to finish her graduate studies and move on, Addison began to think she'd never have an opportunity to, as she wrote, *climb the tower of the great harbor light* she'd admired from a distance for so many years.

Addison's letter said I'd made a positive impression on her mother when I toured the museum, and that Annie didn't impress easily. Addison learned from her mother that I was interested in the history of the lighthouse, and that she possessed an artifact that provided more information about the island. Addison invited me to visit the museum again when I came ashore, and that she'd be home during spring break holiday the second week in March.

She wrote, *I hope you can spare an afternoon in the village. I'd like to buy you lunch and we can talk.* She signed it, *Warmest wishes for the holidays. Stay warm and dry. -- Addison.*"

115

I sat silent, re-reading her letter a second time. Patience was a personal virtue, so I'd call on it to help me stay focused for another eleven weeks. Weather was too unpredictable these days to risk leaving my post, so I had no choice.

Afternoons of gusty winds and sleet-drenching nights were the norm for several days. Colder temps meant less lightning and thunder, but nothing abated the rain. I wore layers of thermal undergarments, wool sweaters and a parka under my slickers. I was still chilled while perched high above the waves, surrounded by the cold steel and brass of the balcony and lamp housing.

Calmer seas and milder temperatures ushered in the New Year. It cleared enough for me to scout the island for debris. I spent several afternoons in the caverns, and on the sandbar at the mouth of the cave. Sunsets were majestic.

Chapter 21

Nightmares

I dreamt I was sailing a sloop in Bellwether Bay on a warm, sunny day. I stood at the helm and kept an eye on the wind in the sheets. Headsail was taut and the jib billowed like a spinnaker on a racing yacht. I had good speed, and more when I trimmed the main. A boat this size needs a crew, but I'm alone, tacking through the waves toward the buoy markers at the mouth of the Bay.

Then the wind shifted, the sails fluttered and the boat slowed. Waves broke over the bow and water spilled into the shallows of the lower deck.

I left the wheel and pulled the mast lines and trim ropes. The boat continued to take on water. The mainsail now hung below the boom, and the jib dragged in the waves on the starboard side.

My boat was sinking.

I managed to turn the bow and the mainsail came to life, but the lines were slack and the boom flew out beyond the railing. The sail needed reefing, but there was no one to tie the lines.

The sky darkened, the boat turned perpendicular to the waves, and water flowed over the bow. Objects in the lower deck floated out of the hatch. In the debris was a life preserver with "Lost Souls" painted on it.

A gale nearly upended the boat. I heard a crack, and the mast splintered and fell back toward me. I raised my arm to block the blow, and then I woke. I sat up in bed.

The storm in my dream was buffeting the walls of my home. I was awake, but I still heard the mast splintering. I rose and stepped out into the hallway and looked over the railing. The noise came from the front entry. The hinges creaked before the door imploded and threw wood shards around the room. I raised my arm to shield my face, just as I'd done in my dream.

The storm spilled through the open door. It brought a deep blue light with it. The light faded as I descended the stairs. I stepped out into the storm in my nightclothes. The tower door across the courtyard was saturated in blue light. The rain was heavy, but the wind was calm. I reached the tower, turned the steel handle and stepped through into the room. I was drenched.

It was dark until the great light above rotated downward and saturated the room. The spiral staircase was silhouetted on the walls. Twenty feet above the floor, directly in front of me, hung a man's corpse. He wore a seaman's coat.

I heard crying, and saw the child on the floor beneath the man. The infant wailed and clawed at the flagstones.

118

Principal Keeper

The entrance to the cave was still open from my recent visit. A blue fog floated over the floor and seeped down into the well. The cap slid, unaided over the hole, and sealed the opening.

The child's cries grew louder and echoed through the tower. I looked up into the face of the seaman. His eyes opened and I stumbled backward through the doorway and fell into the mud. When I looked up, my face was inches from an angry harbor seal. He was probably more afraid of me than I was of him. I jumped up and ran to the house. The door was intact, and not shattered, as I'd seen it before. I bolted it behind me.

I woke a second time, still in my bed. It was another dream. I lay there wondering if all the ghostly visits had been dreams. My interest in Caroline's fate had waned in the weeks since Addison's visit. I'd spent considerable time thinking about when I'd see her in the spring. This latest nightmare reminded me that I shared the island with restless entities: real or imagined. I needed a break from the solitude and isolation. Addison was the best of several reasons to make a trip to the mainland.

I lay awake in the dark until time came to dress, eat and begin chores.

For several days, I woke in a foul mood, but didn't know why. I didn't recall any nightmares, but I felt as if I'd been restless throughout the night. There were no storms, so I did detail work like polishing the chrome and brass fixtures, and washing out the rain gauges. While cleaning the lantern windowpanes, I found writing on

119

the glass, as though someone wrote their name with an oily finger. I read *Luke* and a group of numbers. The smudges dissolved under the cleaning solvent. Perhaps one of the recent visitors to the island scribbled on the glass, and left a cryptic personal message.

Trips into the caves were sporadic and brief. It was damp and cold, so climate in the subterranean world was forbidding and uncomfortable. The view was still pleasant from the mouth of the cave, as I sat on the strip of sand and stared at the choppy sea.

The harbor seals returned to their perch one day, but they didn't regard me as a threat. Nor were they as menacing as the one in my dream. They barked a chorus of "hellos" when I walked by, and reminded me of my desire to find a pet.

Two weeks prior to Addison's spring recess dates, I sent a message to her in care of her mother. The note told her of my plans to adopt a pet when I came ashore. I wrote, *Do you, or your mother, know of someone who has a puppy or parakeet I can adopt?*

I wrote that I planned to take a vacation, that I requested a temporary replacement from the home office, a common practice when a keeper took holiday, and that I'd made reservations at Bellwether's finest resort lodge.

The message was sent via the harbor telegram station. It was a privilege afforded me at the cost of the ministry.

I was surprised when I hadn't heard from Addison or her mother by the second week of March. Perhaps she'd changed her

Principal Keeper

mind about meeting. In fairness, I didn't ask her to respond to my note. I'd still look forward to seeing her when I left the rock.

I spent an afternoon briefing my temporary replacement. Tobias McKinney was genial, a senior gentleman whose wife passed away two years ago. He'd been a principal keeper for a dozen years at another lighthouse before he retired to a farm further inland. When his wife of forty-six years died, Tobias signed on as a temporary for the ministry. Keeper assignments were rare, so he was often called upon to fill in for an inspector or superintendant. He served when called upon, but spent most of his time on the farm.

There was little for me to show or tell him. Tobias was a seasoned keeper. He was an excellent short-term replacement.

Chapter 22

A Death

The launch came early one morning. Tobias and I traded places. He got off, and I got on. We shook hands as we passed on the pier. He didn't bother with the formality of watching the boat depart, but turned around and walked up the slope toward the tower. I was confident that my post was in good hands.

When we reached the harbor, I threw my duffle on my shoulder and walked the quarter mile to the inn where I had reservations for the week. It was a traditional New England-modern style home with tall windows and six uniquely decorated rooms. My suite had a balcony view of the harbor. It was the largest accommodation in the inn.

"We take care of our keeper," the woman at the desk said and smiled when she handed me the key.

I unpacked, cleaned up, and went downstairs to the dining room for breakfast. I returned to the room after to change clothes before heading to the museum.

Principal Keeper

The air was cool, typical of the last weeks of winter. Spring came earlier to other swaths of the country, but not this far north. Chilly conditions lingered longer along the Atlantic northeast. Spring brought flowery days, and it was heaven-like from May to August, with only an occasional storm. Today would be chilly and overcast.

I passed through the gate, took the porch steps two at a time and froze in front of the wreath on the front door. The black flowers obscured the glass panes. I was shocked, and uncertain what to make of this symbol of death and mourning. I opened the door and stepped into the foyer. Everything was just as I'd seen it before. My boot steps echoed in the hallway. I smelled the warm furnace air. I thought I heard movement upstairs, but then there was nothing.

"Hello," I called out. "Annie?" I walked to the archway that led to the parlor.

"Daniel?" a familiar voice called from above.

I stepped back and looked up to the landing. It was Addison.

"What happened? Where's your mother?"

Addison looked at her hands. She touched her palms and massaged her fingers. I knew now why I didn't receive any communication from the Gilberts.

We planned to meet for dinner at the inn. Addison had business at the museum, and I needed time to process the passing of a wonderful, gracious lady. Annie and I had only met once, briefly,

123

but she'd made an impression, it was a memorable visit, and now she was gone.

Addison sat on the overstuffed loveseat in lobby when I came down the stairs. I thought I was early and was surprised to see her waiting. We sat at a window facing the ocean in the dining room. I ordered a micro-brew and she had white wine.

"I'm sorry I didn't answer your letter," she began.

"Please don't be. I understand. I regret not attending your mother's funeral. She was a kind soul. I didn't know her well, but our visit was special. I liked Annie immensely. I hope you had family to help you."

"Mother and I had each other," she said. "Mom also had a wealth of friends here in Bellwether Bay, and they all came to the church. That was a comfort, to know that she was well loved in the village, because I was away so much at school."

The waitress came and took our orders.

"I didn't get your letter until I came home and found it among mother's things. I don't think she had a chance to forward it to me." She ran her fingers along the stem and base of her wine glass. She turned to look at the ocean. "Have you ever noticed how the water turns almost black in the fading light? You can still see it, there's light, but the water turns dark blue, like the color of ink."

I didn't answer. I knew she wanted to talk, needed to talk, and I was smart enough to give her room to open up.

124

"How silly of me. You live in a lighthouse. I imagine you know every color of the sea, from dawn to dusk, in all sorts of weather." She looked at me for the first time since we'd been seated. "Does the sea have many colors, Daniel?" she asked.

"Yes, lots of shades and hues," I told her.

"I appreciate your taking time to meet for dinner. You must get so little time all year to come ashore, and here I am wasting precious moments talking about the ocean, something you know all too well, I suspect." She paused, glanced at me and then turned away. "Please say something," she whispered.

"Nothing could be further from the truth, Addison," I told her. "To spend time with you, even just a dinner, and to talk about the sea … I can't imagine a better way to spend my time here on the mainland."

"You must be starved for human contact after so many months alone," she said.

We were playing a game, judging each other, deciding how far to go, how much to say, what level of personal thoughts and feelings to share. It's like that at the beginning of all new relationships, isn't it? I didn't know how Addison felt about me, other than as a friend. I thought it wise not to seem too eager.

"It isn't lonely out there," I said. "I took the job, in part, to get away from people, not in general, but specific people and situations. Sharing dinner with you is not because I'm starved for human contact. I enjoy life in the shadow of the tower. I don't need to be alone, but traveling solo is the way some people find themselves." I smiled. "Besides, a ghost or two roam the island and keep me company." We laughed. "I'm exactly where I want to be, with the person I want to share my time."

I caught Addison off guard. "You're kind," she said.

"I needed a break from the lighthouse," I told her. "After we met on the island, I looked forward to seeing you again."

"My visit to the Seward Lighthouse meant a lot. I waited a long time to see it up close."

"You can visit any time," I said.

Addison had to know I was attracted to her. What she said next would tell me if she had similar feelings for me. If she continued to refer to me as "kind" or "thoughtful" or some other innocuous compliment, I'd know she wasn't interested. If, however, she changed the conversation or segued to a lighter subject, then she was leaving the door open.

She chose the latter when she said, "I did read your letter, and I think I may have found you a pet." She smiled, and the candlelight in the room flared.

"Really, what kind?"

"It's a dog, but not a mutt," she said. "Please let me name her for you."

"Then it's a female companion I'll take back to the island at the end of the week?"

"Of course." Her smile was even bigger this time.

Here now was more of the beautiful woman who visited the island. Addison was carefree and happy that day, and now her life was solemn and serious. It was great to see again the wonderful personality that captured my heart when we first met.

"It would mean a great deal to me if you named my companion," I said. "What kind of dog is it?"

"A golden retriever, I think. The family that owns the grocery store on Atlantic has pups to give away. They offered me one at the funeral, but I declined. I think they'd be proud to have one living on the island, helping the keeper to keep the light."

I studied how she held her wine glass and the way she touched her lips with the rim. I listened to every word, heard the rise and fall in her voice. How she tilted her head before she delved into a new thought. Addison was a bouquet of nuance. It would be even harder to say goodbye this time.

Our meal came, and with the exception of a word or two, we ate in silence. The world closed in as the sunlight waned and the candlelight grew brighter. She'd smile one moment, and then be deep in thought. Her mother's passing still weighed heavy on her.

"Would you like to take a walk down by the water," I asked.

"You don't think it's too cold?"

"Perhaps ... for you." I smiled. "I live in cold, damp weather."

"And I live in New York, remember? I live on an island, too."

I helped her with her shawl. "This was your mother's, wasn't it?"

"Yes, her favorite. I gave it to her for Christmas one year."

I took her hand as we walked along a wooden pier, a strip of beach below. I put my arm over her shoulder when the wind gusted, and she held my waist.

We walked all the way to the end, where the pier met the Bay, then turned back. Like our dinner, few words were spoken. There were no hesitations, or expectations. We were comfortable together. We shared a bond, a need satisfied by the other's presence.

When we came to the lodge, we returned to the restaurant for Irish coffee.

"Did you drive over?" I asked.

"No, I walked. I rarely use my car in the village."

"Can I walk you home?"

"I'll be fine, thank you. I need to walk a little by myself tonight," she said.

I followed her through the lobby and out the front door. We hugged, and then she pulled her wrap up around her neck and shoulders. When she reached the street, I called out to her.

"Addison. You never told me about the artifact you have, the one associated with the light in the harbor."

"She turned. "Oh, Daniel, I forgot to bring it. That was the purpose of dinner, wasn't it? My mind's been foggy lately."

Principal Keeper

"It's understandable. Does this mean you'll share dinner with me again tomorrow night?" I asked.

"I can't. I have an early flight for a meeting back in the City." She turned to leave, and raised her voice as she moved away. "I'll drop it off at the front desk here on my way to the airport in the morning and we can talk about it when I return."

She walked away.

I watched until she disappeared in the darkness, and then returned to my room. I sat on the balcony and drank a beer. The moon drifted in and out of the clouds. I couldn't see the tower, but I saw its beam cone out across the water to the horizon. It flashed when it turned toward me, and then faded when it moved away. Perhaps it was searching for me.

I thought about Addison and her mother, Annie. Both were confident and strong willed. I knew what it was like to unexpectedly lose a parent, and I was certain Addison could weather her personal storm. I wanted to help her more, but I didn't know if I'd ever see her again.

I closed the French doors and got into bed. It felt strange not to be surrounded by the ocean. The wind outside was gentle and soothing, nothing anything like the howling so prevalent on the island.

I fell into a deep sleep.

I dreamt that the wind blew the balcony doors open. Moonlight filled the room. A figure stood at the foot of my bed, and

129

then moved to stand next to me. A hand touched my brow. I opened my eyes, and then closed them again.

It was only a dream.

Chapter 23

A Gift

I was headed for the dining room when the desk clerk called out to me.

"Mr. Riggs! We have a package for you," the young man said and held up a small box wrapped in brown paper. "There's a note with it."

I took the items into the dining room. The card was from Addison. It read,

I've had this in my possession for a long time. I found it in a secluded space in my mother's house when I was in high school. She let me to keep it, even though it possessed historical significance. I'll donate it to the museum one day.

Inside the box was a leather-bound book. The note continued,

When I first read it, I identified with the author. Her words helped me navigate through an ocean of adolescent tantrums. Maybe that's why mother let me hang on to it.
Happy reading. See you the day after tomorrow. – Addison

I would see her again, soon. That put a smile on my face. I put the book aside, ordered breakfast, then picked it up again. I opened it. The handwritten first line, read,

This is the private diary of Caroline Mackenzie of Parkersburg, Ohio.

It was dated 'September 29, 1929.' I thumbed three-quarters into the pages and read,

Today, March 12, 1931, Colin took Emily to the top of the tower for the first time.

The words hit me like a gale-force wind. I dropped my fork onto the plate. Was it possible that this was the private musings of Caroline Cheswick, a diary she began before her marriage?

I finished eating and went straight to the balcony in my room. It was noon before I stopped reading. I ordered lunch brought up. I needed time to think.

I learned that Caroline was married to John Mackenzie when she began the diary. John was Emily's father, the child discovered on the island when Caroline disappeared and Colin hung himself. Caroline couldn't support herself and the child when John died in a work-related accident, so she married Colin Cheswick, an older man who brought her and Emily to live on the island. Colin was a loving husband who embraced Emily as if she were his own child. His only fault, Caroline wrote in her journal, was that he drank heavily, and

Principal Keeper

became moody and sullen. Caroline kept her distance from Colin during his *spells*, as she called them.

I read that Caroline discovered and explored the caves. She loved the solitude of the deep caverns and the beauty of the beach at the mouth of the giant cave. Her words eloquently expressed my own feelings about the peaceful world beneath the island. It became her subterranean secret garden.

John, her first husband, was the love of Caroline's life. She wrote of her pain at his passing, the emptiness and loneliness she endured. In the years following his death, long after she'd married Colin, she wrote about her undying love for John, the father of their child, Emily. Escapes to the cave were her refuge from the sadness she felt, and to stay away from Colin when he was drinking. Colin never joined her in this place, so it was there that she communed with the memory of her first love. The journal included letters to John, written while she sat on the strip of sand by the ocean. She wrote about their conversations and special moments.

Caroline never let rest the memory of John. Their child was a constant reminder of their marriage and love for each other. Colin's sullenness made her more despondent about losing her first husband. The caves were a place where she felt closer to him, and where she recounted their times together, and the happiness in her life before his death.

She'd done what was necessary to protect herself and her child when she married Colin, but she was filled with guilt about the

133

circumstances that led to her journey to the island and her life with Cheswick. Colin begged Caroline to have a second child, and she may have convinced him that she was pregnant before the tragedy.

I was certain now that Caroline was the ghost, and that Colin Cheswick's spirit was the tortured soul hanging in the tower. The child was Emily Mackenzie, whose cries I heard in the storms. But, what happened to Caroline, and why did she haunt me? The contents of the diary confirmed a lot of suspicions, but there were more questions.

The last entry in the diary was on July 29, 1932. It was a brief entry that read,

Big blow coming, black weather on the horizon. Must check the treasures in the cave before the tide rises. Colin edgy and taken to the bottle. Emily in a foul mood, as well. Tension everywhere, in everyone. Will keep my time in the caves brief.

At the bottom of the page was a reference to biblical scripture, 'Luke 21.32'. The rest of the pages in the diary were blank.

I was anxious to talk to Addison. Perhaps she could add more to Caroline's story. The day was late. The shadows were long. I rose from the balcony chair, set the diary on the nightstand, and left. I needed to walk.

I strolled through town and stopped to look into the windows of the closed shops. When I reached the pier where Addison and I walked the night before, I sat on the dock. The tower light was there,

Principal Keeper

combing over the ocean. Round and round, light, then dark, then light again. The lamp was more than a beacon for errant ships. It was also Caroline's spirit as she searched for her daughter. I was profoundly affected by Caroline's words. Aside from the child that she and John created together, Caroline found it unbearable to live in the ashes of his death.

I pulled up my collar and headed back to the inn. I realized that the appeal of long walks came from months of confinement. I missed my home, but I enjoyed being on dry land for a spell.

I passed Silas's house. The old man was a key to solving the mysteries. I'd always be grateful.

I fell asleep thinking about Addison's return to the village. I bolted upright when it dawned on me that Addison had to know about the caves, assuming she read the diary. The secret was no longer my own to bear. She'd known about them when she visited the island. We'd have much to talk about in the days ahead.

I slept late, and spent the second day shopping. After dinner, I wrote a lengthy passage in my journal, mostly about Addison, and was early to bed. The sooner the day dawned, the sooner I'd see her. It felt a bit like Christmas Eve.

I went to my favorite restaurant for breakfast the next morning. The Chowder Box staff greeted me warmly. I was flattered that patrons, year-round residents of the village, recognized me. The principal keeper was a celebrity in Bellwether Bay. I was the guardian of their iconic lighthouse. I was the person who kept the

135

Frank Pickard

fire burning, and the lamp protected their families from harm. My work touched all of their lives.

When I finished my meal, I thanked the staff, waved to patrons who introduced themselves, and headed across the street to make my way back to the inn. I planned to journal and wait for Addison's call. I stopped in front of the museum, and admired the gingerbread and gables.

"Ye know'd about the light, din't ye?"

The voice came from behind me. I turned and saw Silas in the middle of the street with both hands braced on a cane. "Mr. MacClarin, good morning," I answered.

"Ye know'd about the light, din't ye?" he repeated.

"What light is that, Mr. MacClarin?" I asked.

Silas turned to face the harbor, raised the tip of his cane and pointed. "Out there, in the harbor. You see'd it, din't ye?" He faced me again. "The blue lady, ye saw the blue lady."

I walked toward him. "How do you know about the blue lady?" I asked.

"Ye can't sit on that damn porch o'mine day and night, and not see things, things other people don't notice." He took a step toward the harbor. "She lives out there on the water. Ya figured that out, din't ye? She be a true maid of the harbor, watches after the sailors and ships, you know? She steers 'em away from the shoals and rocks, guides them safely into port. I seen her many times." He turned and grinned at me. "Ye seen a fair bit too, haven't ye?"

136

Principal Keeper

"Where do you think she comes from, Silas?" I had never used his first name, but now we shared a secret.

"Oh, ye know the answer to that one yer-self. Why do you ask me?" He pushed the cane forward and shuffled away. I heard him say, "Ye know'd already. Make's no sense for ye to ask me that question. She haunts ye dreams, now, don't she?"

Silas reached the other side of the street and turned toward his home.

I considered rushing after him, but my attention was drawn to a car that pulled to the curb. It was Addison.

"Daniel, what are you doing here?" she asked through the window.

I motioned toward the old man. "I ran into Silas after breakfast."

Addison got out of the car, took my arm, and together we watched Silas' progress down the street. "He reminds me of a snail," she said. "Slow, but steady. Silas is a gentle soul." She kissed me on the cheek. "Let's get out of the street. I don't want you to get run over in the bustling metropolis of Bellwether Bay," she joked.

We went up the walk and into the museum.

"We have a lot to talk about," I said.

"Yes, we do."

Chapter 24

Revelations

"So you read my diary?" she asked as we walked up the stairs to the third floor of the museum.

"Don't you mean Caroline's diary?"

"Yes, of course. It was in my possession for so many years, and I read it over and over, so often that sometimes I dreamt it was my life, but it isn't my story," she said as she turned down a hallway and entered a room on the right.

I followed her. Construction paper covered the windows, so a dusty brown light hung in the air. I lost sight of Addison in the maze of sepia shadows.

She spoke in whispers in the diffused light. "This was my room when I lived with mother." She rummaged through boxes and shelves. "When I left home, the room was relegated to storage space for our personal possessions." Addison thumbed through a children's book, and grinned. "I dreamt good dreams in this room."

Principal Keeper

Above me was a hexagon cupola with six portals and a ledge. I'd noticed it from the street. Unseen from inside was a widow's walk with iron railing. Fitting that the home of a seafaring man would have a place to survey the open ocean.

"I spent hours up there," she said, and pointed at the cupola. "The ledge is deep enough for a child to sit and gaze at the sea, or the stars. Sort of like the balcony gallery on your tower, isn't it? When the weather was fair, I'd sit outside on the crown, next to the weather vane. In a storm, I was up there, on the shelf, and I'd stare out the portals. I fantasized that it was a crow's nest on a transatlantic schooner. In fact, that's where I discovered the diaries."

"Diaries? There are more of them?" I was shocked.

"I only found one book, but there are entries that refer to at least one more, an earlier account, when Caroline was a young girl." She was quiet, and then changed the subject. "How did you discover the caves?" she asked.

""How did you know I found the caves?" I asked.

"By the look on your face when I stood over the capstone in the tower during the tour, remember?" She found a shoebox filled with photographs. "You were like a child with his hand in the cookie jar. You have an expressive face, Daniel."

It felt as though a weight had been lifted from my shoulders. I sat in a Windsor chair in the corner.

139

She looked up from the photographs. "I wouldn't have told you about the diary if I didn't believe you knew about the caves. I would have kept Caroline's secret. So, how did you find them?"

I had to think. It seemed so long ago. "I spilled tea one morning while climbing the stairs and the liquid melted into the mortar between the stones."

She smiled and nodded. "I suppose that would raise suspicions." Addison set the box of photographs aside and approached. She pulled a pillow from a cardboard box and sat in front of me. She curled her knees up to her chin like a child. "Tell me what it's like down there, please," she begged. "I've wanted to know everything about the caves since the day I first read her story." She waited patiently.

"The caves," I began, "are peaceful. There's a beach, a sandbar at the mouth of a large cavern that opens to the sea. But, you already know that from reading her diary."

"So, it's true. And the mouth of the cavern is below the cliffs, isn't it? I knew it the moment I stood on the rocks above."

"Yeah, it's below the cliff on the lee side of the island, facing the mainland." I stood and walked to the center of the room. "When I first went into the caves, I found driftwood and glass fishing balls, deck chairs and cushions. I took some of the objects back to decorate the cottage.

"And the waxed box?" she asked.

Principal Keeper

I stopped to think. "The what? A box? No, I didn't find a box."

"Then it must still be there," she said.

"Or it washed out to sea," I said. "I would have remembered a box."

"Don't you remember her story about the treasure chest she left in the cave?"

"I thought Caroline was writing about the colorful glass balls and driftwood she found. I didn't think she had a treasure chest," I said.

"Not a treasure, but a metal box coated in wax. She mentions it late in her diary," Addison insisted.

"I returned to the chair and stared down at her. "What's in the box?" I asked.

"Memories, photographs, a locket, maybe another diary, objects from a life before Colin Cheswick, when she was with John," she said. "Would you like to see her?"

Her question startled me. Did she know about the ghostly visits? "You know what she looks like?" I asked.

"Yes, from her picture," she said and stood.

"But there are no pictures in the museum from those years." I rose from the chair. "Your mother and I searched the collection."

"You're correct, there are none on display, and none of Caroline during her years on the island. But ..." she pulled a box from a shelf and opened it, "... there were two photographs in the

141

pages of the diary, taken before she came to Bellwether Bay." She dropped the box and moved her search into the closet. "I used to keep them with other family pictures, in a cigar box." She dug deep beneath the clothes hangers. "You know the kind of box, with a picture of the twelve musketeers, or whatever. It was a box like that." Addison went as far back into the closet as possible, then said, "Here it is!"

She walked back into the room and dropped down onto the pillow. She opened the box and took out a handful of black and white photographs. "These are of mother and me, and then mother after I moved out. I even have a picture of my father somewhere. He was handsome enough, but her, well, she was a looker!" She smiled at a photograph of her mother.

I sat in the Windsor. I was uneasy with the thought of seeing a picture of Caroline. Would it be the same person who haunted the island, or would it be another face? In my mind, Caroline was the restless spirit of the lonely blue lady. To find out otherwise would be disturbing. It had to be her, or I'd be back at the start in my effort to solve the mystery.

"Here they are." She held out two sepia-toned photographs. They were larger than snapshots, maybe four by six. "That's Caroline."

I took them with both hands. The first was a photograph of a young woman leaning against a chestnut tree. A Model T style automobile was in the background. She looked to be in her teens. She could have been younger. I audibly sighed, "It's her."

"Yes," Addison said, but she mistook my meaning.

I hadn't decided when, or if, I'd tell Addison about my encounters with Caroline at Seward Lighthouse. Caroline was no more than a dream until this moment. This was the woman who haunted me. She was real, or had been at one time. She looked innocent, delicate and ethereal. Even in the photograph, Caroline looked to be in her own world.

The blue lady was undoubtedly Caroline Cheswick, but I was also surprised how much Addison resembled the young girl in the photograph, particularly on the day she visited the lighthouse. They were physically alike, and shared similar facial features. High cheekbones, delicate chins, and both had thick, wavy hair. I was drawn to Addison, perhaps, because she was the woman in my dreams.

The second photograph was closer. I saw Caroline's face more clearly. She held an infant, and smiled broadly into the camera lens. This photograph, too, looked like Addison. The child in Caroline's arms was younger, but I was certain it was the same as the spirit who pulled on my bedcovers.

"It looks like you," I said.

"That's what mother said, but I disagreed. There are similarities in our hair and height, but not much else." She took the photograph from my hand and looked at it. "I wanted to be Caroline.

143

I dreamed of being a mysterious, beautiful woman who lived in an age of romance, and who I came to know intimately through her memoirs. Like Caroline, I wanted to meet and marry John, and have children. Morbidly, I even fantasized that I'd live out my life, as she did, forced to marry an older man I did not love, but who could provide for me and my fatherless child, while tragically holding on to the memory of my first, great love. Silly romantic dreams of a young mind." Addison was silent as she stared at the photograph. "It sounds absurd, even in this room where I had all those daydreams."

I started to respond, but wisdom cautioned me to stay silent.

She sifted through the pictures of family and friends. "Ah, Mary Hayes, my best friend through junior high and high school. We had lots of sleepovers in this room. Her father was abusive and drank heavily, so she often stayed with us." She held out a photograph. "Here's a picture of mother at my graduation." She moved and sat next to me.

"Annie was beautiful, Addison," I told her.

"Everyone liked her. She had a slew of friends. I admired her for a lot of reasons, but mostly for the way she raised me. I never felt cheated, not having a father around. She was so damn smart. There were more brains and toughness in her than anyone I knew. I never saw her cry, or complain, or lose her temper. She disciplined me when necessary, but she never scolded. She'd tell me I'd made a mistake and that I needed to fix it. She spoke with conviction and with so much truth that no one questioned her."

Principal Keeper

"Like you," I said.

I couldn't see her face, but I knew she was crying. She used her free hand to wipe tears from the corner of her eyes.

"I could not have asked for a better parent," she said.

"I'm sure that's true, Addison. You were lucky to be her child." I placed my hand on her shoulder. "I'm certain Annie was proud when you left and cut your own path."

"I missed her when I left for Columbia, and then I moved permanently to the City. She encouraged me to spread my wings. She understood that I inherited her strength and independence." Addison looked up at me. "I may have avoided relationships because mother taught me to live alone, to be independent." She smiled. "I did have one wild impulsive spell with a graduate student soon after I left home, but that's another story."

"That's a lonely existence, Addison. Take it from someone who knows."

"How do you do it? You don't seem to mind your isolation," she said.

"I wasn't always alone. I have a history of marriage and starting a family, a life, an existence far removed from Bellwether Bay and the Seward Lighthouse." I paused. "It was another time, long ago. I never imagined that my life would lead me here, to this place and the job on the island." I glanced around the room.

"What happened to bring you here, Daniel?" she asked.

145

I began slowly. "I created a perfect life. I had the job, the income, the beautiful and intelligent wife and child, and a house in the 'burbs'. My wife was active in Junior League and our son played in soccer tournaments. I had everything. My life was perfect."

"Then?" she asked.

"Then, just as quickly, it disappeared." I stood and walked to the middle of the room. She moved into my vacated chair. "I made mistakes that hurt people. Good, honest people."

"You were a banker?" she asked.

"Investment broker. I was successful. When I finished my graduate degree, my father-in-law hired me at the brokerage firm he co-founded. I got the job on my own merits and track record. I wouldn't have it any other way." I touched the edge of a lace shawl spilling from a garment box on the shelf. The fabric was yellowed with age. "My story is common," I continued. "I made risky investments that went sour. I invested too quickly and people lost their savings, their retirement funds. My rush to amass large trades ruined a lot of people."

"You were doing your job by investing money your clients gave you to invest," she said. "Isn't that what it means to broker?"

"The difference is that I lost sight of the people I was trying to help. I got greedy. I felt pressured to make money, to take bigger risks." I stood in front of her now. "There were plans for a house in the country, an expensive private school for our son, helping to fund the charities my wife supported, and her exorbitant spending. I

Principal Keeper

worked harder, and I made riskier trades. The money was great and I thought it'd all slow down, and I'd take my foot off the pedal before anyone was hurt. But the bigger gains put more pressure on me to keep going. Then the market dropped, hard, overnight, and people who counted on me began to loose their shirts, and homes, and yachts. Including my wife's family."

"Didn't anyone stand by you, help you out of the mess?" she asked.

"My marriage was shaky. I fell short of my wife's expectations. She was involved in community action groups and political campaigns. When my mistakes went public and hit the press, she accused me of soiling her reputation."

"Daniel, you never meant to hurt anyone," she said.

"Doesn't matter, Addison. I bought into the rush, the lifestyle. I took the risks.
My father-in-law was squeezed out of his own firm because of me. He came home one night, closed the garage door and went to sleep with the engine running." I cleared my throat. "Carl was a good man who treated me with respect. His suicide destroyed what was left of my marriage."

"Daniel, I'm so sorry," she said and moved toward me.

"She told our son that I killed his grandfather. I couldn't find work in my field, moved out of my home, and eventually came north. I stopped running when I took the principal keeper job."

She put her hand on my shoulder.

147

"Last contact I had with my wife and son was when her lawyer served me divorce papers. That was three years ago."

Addison put her arms around me and we held each other. She put her lips to my ear and whispered. Her words were supportive, and cryptic. "It's time to turn a page. The book is written, Daniel," she said. "You need to face your demons. Events have been put into motion and we only have to wait for things to happen in their proper time and order. The plan for our lives was mapped out before we were born. We can't stop it. Someday you'll see that I'm right. I was unsure until I visited the island and met you. Now, I'm certain."

She said no more, and I didn't ask questions. I only took her word for it.

Chapter 25

A Companion

We left the museum and walked to the inn for lunch. It was a sweet feeling not to be alone any longer. Addison turned a new page in my life. She moved my story forward. I felt whole for the first time in years with her by my side.

"It's time to retrieve your child," she said as I signed the lunch invoice.

"My child?" I asked.

"Your new companion, your comrade in duty," she said. "Your pet, the golden retriever. Remember?"

"My new resident on the rock, of course. Have you thought of a name?" I asked.

"I have, but let's look at the litter first. I want to see if the name fits."

She led me further up the street than I'd ever ventured. It felt as though we were leaving the village limits, headed for the highway, up into the forested hills surrounding Bellwether Bay. We approached the *Now Entering* sign at the edge of town. Below the seals of civic organizations were the words, *Founded in 1799*, and below that, *Home of the World Famous Bellwether Bay Harbor Light.*

We crossed the road and walked up a graveled driveway. At the end, nestled in the spruce and pine was a modest board-and-batten home with a bay window that faced the harbor.

"I thought you said they owned a gas station or store, something like that." We approached the house.

"The Baileys own the station and the store. This is the home of their son, Cletus and his family." She led the way.

We heard barking. A screened door swung open and a big fellow stepped onto the porch. He wore gray slacks with red suspenders over a white shirt. He pushed his hands into his pockets and assumed a Paul Bunyan-like stance as the door slammed behind him. Cletus Bailey looked as though he'd just come from breakfast and was ready to start his day. He didn't wear a coat or hat, which seemed unwise in the cold morning air, but I'd heard about these hearty souls who lived their entire lives in the village. The cold never bothered them.

"Mornin' to you Cletus," Addison called out.

Cletus nodded his head and spat in the dirt below the porch.

"Have any more of those pups left from Sally's litter?" she asked.

"Aye, got a few."

Principal Keeper

Cletus came down the porch steps, turned and walked toward the back of his home. He was out of sight when we turned the corner, but Addison knew where to go. In a corner of the storage shed, behind a mower and a table with machine parts and oilcans, was an enclosure of pine boards. Four creatures tumbled around in a pile of quilts.

"The bitch done left 'em to go eat on the back porch. She's been venturing out more these last coupla' days," he said. Cletus stood stoic, hands in his pockets, and stared down into the box.

Addison knelt and picked up a puppy. I looked at Cletus. He seemed detached from the fate of the litter. Like many New Englanders I'd met, Cletus was unemotional about his animals. Natives were not known to wax philosophic about the beauty of the rugged countryside, or see poetry in their harsh existence. Farm animals, too, served a functional purpose. Their lives were measured by the value of their contribution to their master's livelihood. Farm dogs needed to herd and chase away intruders, and alert farmers of predators in the hen house. Otherwise, they were useless.

As I contemplated Cletus' indifference to the puppies, caring little whether they were adopted or drowned in the Bay, the man bent at the waist and picked up a puppy. It was nearly invisible in his large hands. He raised it up close to his face, eye level.

"Well, look at this runt this mornin'. Getting' big, ain't ya?" Cletus coughed and lowered his hands when he saw us looking at him. "I might keep this'un for the kids," he said.

151

Addison turned her attention to the creatures. They welcomed her interest and stumbled over to greet her. She finger-nuzzled a particular pup.

"Golden labs are they, Cletus?" she asked.

"Aye, some lab, a bit of golden, a smidgen of collie. Mostly retriever. Make a good rock and tower dog, any one of 'em," he said and looked at me.

"Yes, I imagine they would," I said.

"This one, Daniel," Addison said. "This one is for us." She picked up the wiggly creature and stepped back from the enclosure. The pup struggled to escape her grasp. There was nothing special about this particular one that warranted Addison's decision.

"Seems a bit unruly," I said when I reached out to pet the dog.

"Exactly. She has a strong will and independent nature. She'll be an able-bodied companion for your lonely existence out on the water," she said.

It didn't escape me that Addison used the term "us" when she chose the dog, but now she spoke of my life alone on the island.

"How much for the dogs, Mr. Bailey?" I asked.

"Gaw. I din't thin' to sell 'em," he said and stared down at the pup in his hands. "Jus' int'rested in findin' each a good home, 's all." He set his puppy down. "Couldn't think to charge ye, Mr. Riggs. Naw't the keeper of the light." Cletus smiled for the first time.

Principal Keeper

"Thank you, Mr. Bailey. I'll give her a good home." I turned to Addison. "I assume it's a 'her'."

"It is," she said and held the animal to her cheek.

"What will you name her, Mr. Riggs," Cletus asked.

"I've left that chore to Ms. Gilbert," I told him.

"Her name's 'Maggie'." She stared down at the fur ball cradled in her arms. My mother's middle name was 'Margaret'.

I was pleased with Addison's gesture. It was a perfect name. "Hello, Maggie." I said and petted the dog. "Thank you, Addison."

We thanked Cletus again, and headed down the drive and up the main road back into town. Addison carried Maggie for the entire journey.

"I'll keep her at my place until the end of the week," she said, if that's all right. The inn might not appreciate an unbroken puppy running through their halls."

When we came to the inn, I asked, "Do you mind if I leave you here? I'd like to rest before dinner. You'll have dinner with me, won't you?"

"No," she said.

"No, you won't have dinner with me?" I asked.

"No, I don't mind leaving you to rest, and, yes, I'd like to have dinner with you," she said.

I petted the fur ball, who was now asleep in Addison's arms, then turned up the path toward the lobby. "I'll pick you up at six-thirty," I said over my shoulder. "If that works for you.

"See you then," and she walked away.

I entered the inn and started up the staircase. I glanced down into the lobby. A young woman stood in front of the windows that faced the Bay. Her arms were folded behind, at her waist. She appeared to be transfixed on the view. Her dark hair fell over her shoulders and down her back. She wore a full-length sundress, and her form was silhouetted against the light in the window. It was an attractive, touristy-sort of picture.

It had taken a couple days to relax and enjoy my time in Bellwether Bay. The image of the girl by the windows and the special moments with Addison coalesced to quiet my mind. The burden of being principal keeper of the lighthouse, as well as the otherworldly occurrences, seemed distant. The peace I sought when I planned this trip descended upon me and lightened my soul.

Chapter 26

The Dark Lady

I fell asleep quickly in the quiet of my room at the inn. I dreamt that Addison and I walked along a New York City street. It was late afternoon. We arrived at our favorite restaurant and chose a table on the patio, next to French doors that opened to the street. European style dining, I thought.

A waiter seated us. We ordered espresso and Danish. Our conversation was light and familiar, as though we'd known each other for years. We held hands across the table.

I glanced over Addison's shoulder and saw a young woman facing away from us. She stood at the curb with her hands clasped behind her in a familiar pose. Her dark hair fell over her shoulders and down her back. Was it the same person I saw by the windows in the lobby? How did she know I'd be here with Addison? Was it coincidence, or was the woman following me?

I stood up and moved toward where the woman waited to cross the street.

"Daniel? What is it?" Addison asked. She touched my arm as I passed.

I got closer to the stranger. I wanted to know why she was following me. The traffic light changed and she stepped off the curb. People crossed toward me, and blocked my path. I struggled to reach her. She melded into the crowd. Then I heard tires squeal. Someone screamed, the crowd parted, and the woman was now face down in the street. I knelt beside her. Her arms were outstretched as though she were floating on the asphalt. The crowd and traffic vanished. We were alone. The skin on her hands was torn and bleeding. I touched her back. Her dress was soaked with water. I began to turn her over, but a loud sound, like a fire alarm bell, startled me. The ringing continued until I drifted awake and took the phone receiver from the cradle next to my bed. The room was dark.

"So, are we having dinner tonight or next week?" Addison asked over the phone.

I was disoriented. The emotions I felt in the dream lingered. "Addison? I'm sorry. I lost track of time," I told her.

"I could be mistaken, but I thought you mentioned dinner at six-thirty," she said. "We can make it later if you like, or tomorrow, even."

I sat up. "No. I just woke from a nap. I didn't mean to sleep this long, but I guess I was more tired than I thought." I rubbed my eyes. "Where are you?"

"In the lobby, but I can come back later."

"It's okay. I owe you an apology for standing you up. Give me a second to change and I'll be down."

I washed my face and changed clothes. I paused at the top of the stairs and studied Addison. She sat, hands folded in her lap, legs crossed, facing away from me, in a winged chair in the middle of the lobby. Her hair was pulled back and pinned. She had an air of sophistication, a quiet elegance. She wore a cotton dress, and a silk scarf draped over her shoulders. She sat motionless, watching people come and go from the gift shop and restaurant. She smiled politely and waved when someone noticed her waiting.

I spoke before she saw me. "I'm so sorry to keep you waiting. I was having the best sleep I've had in months," I told her.

"Then I'm sorry I interrupted your rest," she said, then stood and took my arm.

We moved together toward the dining room. "I'm glad you did. I wanted to see you. I was deep in a dream and would have slept through our date if you hadn't called."

"I hope your dreams were pleasant." She smiled.

"They started pleasant enough, but when you called and woke me ... well, it was good timing." We paused at the hostess desk. "I didn't give much thought to where we'd go tonight. Is there another place you like to dine?" I asked.

"Have you been to The Cottage?" she asked.

"No. Is it near?"

"A short drive. Come on," she pulled me along.

157

Her car was parked outside. I assumed she drove over when I didn't show up at the museum on time. The road led north, past Cletus' place where we found the puppies, past the old mill camp and beyond the water treatment plant, hidden in a stand of pines and sycamores.

We climbed a winding mountain road. The woods were thick. Addison navigated around the narrow turns and switchbacks until we reached the top, where a two-storied house rose in a clearing. It was nearly dark, but every room of the home was lit. Light from the windows spilled into the parking lot and onto the skirt of the surrounding forest.

"It was the private residence of a prominent family fifty years ago," Addison said as she parked. "Now it's a restaurant owned by a semi-retired chef and his family."

"Semi-retired?"

"Paul was head chef for an exclusive restaurant in Largo, Florida, for a decade. Phyllis, his wife, sold high-end real estate. They retired in their mid-forties, moved here and opened The Cottage."

We got out and walked toward the wrap-around porch and entrance.

"That's a new one: Floridians moving north to retire," I said and held the door.

The interior was warm and welcoming. There were wonderful smells of cooked vegetables, seared meats and seafood, baked bread, and something that resembled spicy hot apple cider. A lanky fellow dressed in a white cotton waistcoat stepped from behind a counter to greet us. He resembled an undertaker, with droopy eyes, a long face and tight lips.

"Hello, Paul," Addison said and extended her hand from beneath her shawl.

"Ms. McHenry, how good to see you in The Cottage." He bent at the waist when he took her hand. "We were sad to hear about your lovely mother's passing."

"Thank you." She turned to face me. "Paul, this is Daniel Riggs."

"Well, it's seldom that we have the honor of the company of the principal keeper of the light, the bright bastion that illuminates our harbor waters." He shook my hand and did his waist-bending. "Table for two?"

"Yes, by the fireplace, if possible. It's chilly tonight," Addison said, and followed Paul across the room.

"For you, anything, my love," Paul said over his shoulder. He smiled when they came to their table. His large teeth matched his long face and high forehead.

Paul's demeanor was overly polite, but his admiration for Addison was genuine. He reminded me of a furniture salesman, the type that ran barking at my heels when I accompanied my wife on her shopping excursions. Addison noticed my scrutiny of her friend.

We sat on the far side of the room, against the stone mantel of the fireplace. Only a few tables were occupied, but there appeared to be adjoining dining rooms. Paul handed us menus and rushed away to greet a party who came through the front door.

"Hello, hello, hello everyone. Welcome to The Cottage," we heard him say.

"He's a good cook," she said in Paul's defense, and spread the napkin in her lap.

"I'll take your word," I told her. "He called you 'McHenry'. Are you certain he remembers you?"

"My name was McHenry, once, a long time ago, and only briefly," she said and opened her menu.

"You were married?"

"In an alternate reality, yes. I had a month-long crush on a graduate lab assistant when I was a sophomore. Free spirited personalities were 'the thing' when I was an undergraduate. Mother raised me to think independently and I was mature for my age. I was in love, but love wasn't a requisite for matrimony in those days. I thought our union would last forever, similar tastes, similar interests, a shared love of reading and learning. It was that sort of connection. We didn't know each other, but our stars crossed and we were convinced we were meant to be together. Getting married was easy. No pressure, no hassle, no problem." She paused to sip her water. "After the deed, Gene and I came here to Bellwether Bay to announce our union to mother. Paul and Phyllis had just opened the

160

restaurant and we came here for dinner. I told them years ago that I'd divorced and taken back my maiden name, but the news didn't register. I come here so seldom, so it doesn't matter."

A waiter came, took drink and food orders and disappeared. Addison said that the seafood was always well prepared, so I ordered a lemon-spiced salmon with Caesar salad and baked potato. She ordered a spinach salad, chowder and a grilled chicken entrée.

"How did Annie take the news of your being married?" I wanted to know.

"Mother? Very well. She couldn't resist asking the state of my motherhood." She anticipated my question when she said, "No, I wasn't pregnant. Didn't have plans to ever have children. I was on a mission to be an independent, self-reliant businesswoman. It was a new concept of the time. If that didn't work out, I wanted to save whales or dolphins or wolves. Work with the environment. Marriage was convenient, a weekend diversion. It didn't threaten to cramp my ambitions."

"Funny," I said, "I've never thought of you as impulsive."

"I'm not anymore, but college was a wild time. I was capable of making lots of mistakes during those years."

"So marriage was a mistake?" I asked.

"To Gene, yes. When I was only nineteen, double yes," she said.

I ran my hand over the rough fireplace stones. They reminded me of my home on Seward Island, and the bleached

161

granite walls of the tower. These rocks were more of the riverbed variety, different than the sharp-edged rocks along the ocean cliffs.

"Just when I think I'm beginning to know you, I learn something new," I said.

"Keeps it interesting, doesn't it?" she told me. "You were married once."

"True, but I wasn't young and impetuous about it." I sipped my wine. "There was a long courtship. We took time to get to know each other. Meet the parents, and such."

"Was it a mistake?" she asked.

"No, and not when you consider we had a beautiful son." More diners arrived. The room was getting crowded. The noise level increased.

I wasn't certain how much more to share with Addison. The events in my former life were my pains to bear, but telling her my past would engender trust. "A beautiful son I never see anymore," I said. "He's somewhere in the deep recesses of a crowded, cold city." I looked into her green eyes. Would she understand and empathize, I wondered. "I don't want to trouble or burden you with my personal history."

"I'm here, Daniel. I don't have plans to be anywhere else. I want you to feel free to tell me anything. I wouldn't want it any other way between us."

Principal Keeper

"Nor would I," I said. "You know what bothers me most? I don't know if my son knows I exist. If he does, what does he think of me? Does he think I abandoned him and his mother?"

"You'll have to ask him someday," she said. "I'm sure that, one day, he'll come looking for you and you can explain everything."

The waiter returned with our dinners and we were silent. Everything Addison said made perfect sense. She spoke with conviction, and left doubt in the dust.

I was discovering the depth and definition of the woman who sat across from me. I sensed there was much more to learn. In that moment, I desired nothing greater than to know everything about her. There wasn't a question of falling in love with her, because I was already there. Did she have similar feelings? Addison was so subtle and reserved in her actions that it was hard to tell.

She spoke without looking up from her food, "Eat your dinner, Daniel," she said, and then raised her eyes to mine and smiled.

"I was just ...," I began.

"Yes, Daniel, I know," she said.

Somehow, in some way, I knew that she did.

Chapter 27

Secrets Revealed

After dinner, our conversation returned to the diaries. I felt certain that Addison knew more and held back secrets to unlocking the mystery of the blue lady. She wasn't divulging everything she'd discovered in Caroline Cheswick's diaries.

I was equally guilty. I'd been silent about the ghostly visits. I wanted to tell her, but I didn't want Addison to think that my isolation on the rock had driven me mad. I wanted nothing to come between us now, and revelations about poltergeist children and hanging corpses could damage our relationship.

"You have to understand," she began. "When mother and I moved to the village, I romanticized about the tower and the mysterious island. I recall afternoons walking home from school with friends and we'd stare at the lighthouse on the horizon, and we'd sit for what seemed like hours and make up fairy tales about the families who lived there. We'd dream of spending a night on the island. There wasn't much to capture our imaginations in Bellwether

Bay. The idea of being on the island, alone, surrounded by the ocean, cut off from everyone, was intoxicating. That was heady stuff for a gaggle of love-starved teenagers." She finished her wine. "See, I dreamt of growing up and becoming you."

Her comment made me laugh out loud. "Then you know why it appeals to me."

"My friends and I picked the cutest boy in school, usually Billy Bergfeld, and imagined what it would be like to be stranded out there, all alone, with him." She was lost for a moment in her memory. "My visit to the island last fall was a special day for me."

"Why did you wait so long to visit the lighthouse?" I asked.

"Tours weren't allowed when I was growing up, and only now at the invitation of someone like the district superintendant. Mother also discouraged me from going to the island. There were stories of kids sneaking onto the rock at night, and mother said she'd kill me if I ever dared."

"You're welcome anytime," I said, "at the invitation of the principal keeper, who I understand is an influential person. That's what everyone says. He can even get you a free puppy when you need one, or a choice lobster at the local eatery," I joked. "How's Maggie dog, by the way?"

"Loud," she said.

"Barks?"

"No. Cries. I think she misses her siblings." Her smile morphed into a thoughtful expression. "I want very much to return to

165

the island and visit the caves, now that I know they actually exist. I want to see Caroline's secret place. And I want to look for the box, which I believe is still there."

"Addison …," I began.

"Daniel, if the caves she wrote about are real, why would she lie about a box with her personal treasures?"

I didn't have an answer. "You'll have to explore it for yourself, then," I said and felt it was inevitable, regardless. "When you do, I think you'll agree that it's highly unlikely anything remains hidden in the caves after all these years, given the extent of the flooding at high tide in a storm."

I wanted to press her further on the subject of Caroline's memoir. "What else can you tell me about the contents of the diaries, and the author herself."

"I only know of the existence of a single diary, the one I found in the loft at the museum and shared with you. But there were illusions, passages, that hinted there is at least one more, an earlier memoir. I suspect it documents times that she and John were together, when she was Caroline MacKenzie, before and after the birth of Emily."

The waiter took our plates and returned with coffee. Paul checked on us when he came to stoke the fire next to our table.

The drive down the mountain was slower. We'd round a curve and a half moon would peek through the trees. When the trees thinned and we approached the highway, fingers of lightning reach all the way to the ocean. I thought about the island, and the winding metal steps in the tower, and how the waves sometimes broke over the dock and onto the shore. I was confident in my temporary replacement, but I still thought about my life at the Seward. I considered it my island, my lighthouse. I'd left my child in the care of a skilled babysitter. That's how it felt.

Addison appeared to be mesmerized by the winding road ahead. She'd made my holiday visit special. Our time was brief, but unforgettable, as though we opened a door that would change everything, for both of us.

"I want to visit the island again, Daniel," she said as we approach the village.

"I'd like that," I told her.

"I want to visit the caves," she said. "I want to see Caroline's secret world. Maybe I'll find her treasure."

"How will you feel if you discover that Caroline's treasure is nothing more than driftwood and colored glass washed in from the sea? Will you be too disappointed?" My words sounded harsh, but I worried that reality would be unkind to her.

"Where's the other diary, Daniel?"

"You think it's down in the caves after all these years?" I asked.

"Her later writings ended up in the commodore's home. Probably brought there with other records collected on the island when they discovered the tragedy. The first diary wasn't in that collection. It must still be on the island."

"Maybe she left it behind when John died, before she married Colin and came to Bellwether. Maybe members of her family kept her private things." Addison's shoulders slumped. "The caves flood in a storm," I said, "and I haven't found any place where she could hide something that wouldn't eventually wash out to sea."

Addison was silent. I felt guilty about discouraging her dream. Finding a second diary, if it existed, was important to her, and I'd thrown up roadblocks. "Come and see for yourself. You've known about the caves for a long time. You need to visit." I told her.

I drove into the parking lot in front of the inn, pulled into a space and turned off the engine. Addison stared out the window as raindrops dotted the glass.

"Maybe it's not good to hope," she said. "Maybe the dream is better than reality. She turned to look at me. "Who else knows about the caverns beneath the tower?"

"They were undisturbed for a very long time when I found them. Possibly no one knows about them, except you and I. Silas said Caroline's body was never found, but he didn't say anything about whether anyone looked under the tower. The laborers who built it must have known, but their secret probably died with them, and no one knew about the space beneath the tower until Caroline discovered it. We may be the only ones alive who know about the caves."

Principal Keeper

Lightning moved inland. We heard thunder now. The moon was gone, consumed by invisible clouds.

"When I first told mother about the contents of the diary, she said that it was just the vivid imagination of a lonely, young woman caught in a marriage of convenience to a man twice her age."

"But you believed the caves were there?" I said.

"Yes. I did. It was a formative time in my youth, a time when young girls have romantic daydreams about lost and unrequited love, secret gardens and hidden treasure. That's powerful stuff for a young girl rushing into womanhood. But, I grew up, where dreams are left behind for more adult concerns."

"And now?" I asked.

"I visited the island. I stood over the stone. I saw your face," she said.

"Then it's time you came to Caroline's secret world," I told her.

Chapter 28

Addison's Lighthouse

We sat in a corner of the lobby next to the windows facing the harbor. Lightning strikes illuminated the boats in the harbor.

"Addison," I began, "I return to work the day after tomorrow. We're coming into a quiet time of the year, weather-wise, so maybe I can visit a couple times each month."

"That'd be nice," she said.

The tone in her voice concerned me. I wondered if my occupation would bring an end to our relationship? We'd had so little time together. We were both testing the water, but neither of us signaled a commitment to the other.

"Daniel, will you walk me home?" she asked.

We rose together and crossed the lobby. Neither of us spoke as we walked along the dark streets. She went up the steps of the museum, and left the door open behind her. I didn't hesitate. She turned on the entry light. Shadows stretched upward into the dark corners of the second and third floors. Addison wandered into another room. I wondered what it would be like to live in a museum, surrounded by the images and possessions of past generations. It was a repository for thousands of items that held the energies of their former owners. Pieces of their souls resided in these treasures. The strongest heart would be challenged to live here alone.

Her voice came out of the darkness. "Let's watch the storm from the tower room, my tower, not yours." Addison stood in the half-light of the landing. She turned and started up to the second floor. Lightening flashes through the windows silhouetted her as she moved up toward the third floor. I doubled my steps to catch up.

She turned at the top and headed down the hallway, and then disappeared into the room. I stood in the doorway when a flash threw her shadow onto the floor in the middle of the room. I looked up. She was on the ledge, watching the storm through a portal.

I climbed up and sat opposite her in the cupola. This was the lighthouse of her childhood, I thought. Instead of light radiating outward, it came inward through these windows. How often, I wondered, had light from my tower reached this room, where Addison kept her dreams and secrets hidden.

"My whole life I chose to walk near the water's edge, where waves erased my footsteps. Maybe that doesn't explain it." She began again. "I chose not to leave traces, whether it was my marriage, friends, jobs, even mother to some extent. Why did I do that?" she asked. She turned her eyes to her hands. The sound of thunder grew louder. The storm would soon pass over us.

"Mother's death," she began again, "I don't know. It's important, isn't it? I mean that's what life is about, right? Leaving something behind, memories, friends, a positive mark on someone's life."

I waited, and then began slowly. "Addison, most people are cursed to never see their footprints washed away. They look back and see mistakes, imperfections. Positives in the journey are lost to memory, but the pain and suffering is felt, and stays with them, etched in the sand. The tide never rises high enough to wipe it away." I moved closer to her. "People often can't let go of the ugly moments, or their mistakes. They walk higher on the beach because they want to dwell on the past which only keeps them from moving forward."

It dawned on me that we had traveled in different directions, but our roads led to this place and time. Now we stood together on the same path. The question was, would we go our separate ways, or travel on together.

She leaned against me and we held each other for an hour or more. Rain lashed the windows and thunder rattled the rafters. I felt her body shake. This was the moment Addison chose to grieve for her mother.

Rain was still falling when we left the cupola. The thunder moved further inland. Addison wrapped her arms around me and rested her head on my shoulder as we walked down the hallway. She led me into a bedroom with a cherry wood armoire against one wall,

Principal Keeper

and a cold fireplace with a stone mantel, opposite. There was a walnut four-poster. A dressing room and bath were visible through an open door at the far end of the room.

Addison closed the door leading to the hallway. "This was my mother's room," she said, "then it was mine, and now it's ours."

Chapter 29

A Chance Meeting

I walked up the deserted street. A fog rolled in and gathered around my ankles. I entered the lobby and stood in the stillness of the early morning calm. The nightshift was still at their post.

Music stopped me on the stairs. I thought my weary mind was imagining it, but I heard piano music coming from a room beneath the stairs. I stepped back to the lobby and followed the sound. It stopped, and then began again. It grew louder as I walked down a hallway that opened into a ballroom. Crimson serpentine drapes hung from floor-to-ceiling windows. In the far corner was a piano. A young woman sat at the keyboard, playing. Her hair cascaded over her shoulders and down her back in a familiar pose.

The tune was resonant, and pulled me into the room. I walked toward her. She leaned into the keyboard, and then rocked back as she played. Then I stood with one hand on the piano, just above the soundboard. Surely she knew I was there, but continued to play. Her eyes never rose from the keys. She finished the tune and rested her hands in her lap.

"Such a beautiful tune. What is it called?" I asked, but she didn't respond.

She rose from the bench and stepped away.

"Sorry, I didn't mean to startle you." She looked familiar. "Have we met before, somewhere in the village perhaps?" I asked, but got no response.

She turned toward the door to leave. I touched her shoulder.

"I'm sorry. I didn't mean to alarm you."

She studied my face, and then smiled, took my hand and led me out, back to the lobby. A desk attendant emerged from the back office and began to work at the counter. The woman took a pen from the desk and wrote on the back of a piece of hotel literature. She handed the paper to me.

"*Animabus Damnatis*," I read. "Is that the name of the tune you were playing?" I asked, but when I looked up, she was halfway to the stairs. She reached the landing and turned out of sight. I looked at the paper, *Animabus Damnatis*, and it struck me. I called out, "Wait! How did you know the name of the sailboat in my dreams?

"Sir!" the desk clerk admonished. "Please keep your voice down. Guests are still sleeping."

"Who was that woman?" I asked.

"I didn't see her," he said.

175

"And the piano music?"

"We don't allow people to play the piano this early in the morning," he said.

✳✳✳

I rose early, surprised that I felt rested, since I went to bed so late. It was my last full day shore-side and I wanted to make the most of it. Most importantly, I wanted time with Addison. It was painful to think I'd leave tomorrow and return to my isolation on the island. We planned to meet for an early lunch, shop, and then she promised to take me south for a sunset dinner at a lodge further down the coast.

I walked to the harbor to watch the fisherman. The sand below the pier was hard packed by the rain. I thought about Addison's analogy of life and walking too close to the water. Where had I spent my life, I wondered. Near the water or high up on the shore?

Commercial fishing boats launched before sunrise and were already well past the breakwater. A few boats trolled the harbor for schools of smaller fish. I overheard at dinner the night before that fish "ran deep in the early spring chills", so I questioned how successful the fishing was closer to shore. Heavy rain might bring the fish to the surface to feed, however.

Principal Keeper

My fishing experience extended no further than stream trout and lake bass. I knew nothing about the deepwater sport that was the livelihood of many in the village.

I sat on the dock and watched the gulls and pelicans. Retired folk lined the railing, cutting bait and casting lines into the water below the pier. The birds hovered and waited for the anglers to throw aside their fish heads and guts, and then they swooped in like a rugby team scrambling for a fumbled ball.

The sun warmed the air, and the stench of rotting bait grew pungent. I started back up the shore and came to the cross street that led to the museum. I took the front steps in twos, and knocked. I knocked again and rang the doorbell, but there was no answer.

"Surely she's not still asleep," I whispered.

I reached for the bell again and saw the note taped next to it. *"Had errands. Be back soon. Addison."*

I folded the note and put it in my pocket. I walked along the porch and sat in the swing. Town folk passed, smiled and waved. I measured time by the sun's rays inching over the boards. Twenty minutes later she came up the street. She was radiant and just as beautiful in her summer dress as the day she visited the island. Her smile was warm and her eyes caught the sunlight. She cradled a package, and a strap was draped over her arm. When Addison turned at the gate, I saw Maggie trotting along on a new leash.

"Good morning," she said as she came up the steps. The pup's legs were too short to negotiate the risers, so Addison scooped her up and set her on the porch.

"Yes it is," I said when she kissed me.

She sat next to me. "I have a gift for you," she said and handed me the package. I removed the wrapping and opened the box. Wrapped in tissue was an antique frame with a sepia-toned photograph; the one of Caroline Cheswick that Addison showed me the day before.

"It's my favorite of her," Addison told me.

"Addison, I can't take this ...," I said.

"Please, I know how important the history of your lighthouse is to you, and this is a part of me, my history. I want you to have it," she insisted.

"Thank you. It means a lot. More than I can express," I told her.

"Besides," she began, "you should have a photograph of the souls who haunt you at Seward Lighthouse." Addison stood and walked over to lean on the railing. She turned and smiled.

"You know!" I said, shocked.

"Know what?" she asked.

I realized from the look on her face that her remark was innocent, that she didn't know about the strange occurrences on the island.

"Nothing," I said. I looked at the framed picture. "It's a wonderful gift, Addison. Thank you very much," I said, but I also saw that she was intrigued.

"You don't mean to say ..." Her expression froze. "It isn't ...," she began again. "Daniel, you don't think ..." The impact of my revelation crossed her face and her eyes widened. "It is ..." she began again and decided to phrase it in a question. "Is it haunted, Daniel?" she asked, breathless. She sat down next to me.

"No, I was kidding," I said.

"No you weren't! You're serious!" She grabbed my shoulders and turned me to face her. "What ... who is it, Daniel? What have you seen out there? Are the rumors true?"

I couldn't keep the secret. Her excitement, and insistence, convinced me that Addison wouldn't permit me to keep her in the dark.

So I told her everything. She sat quietly, listening.

"And she always comes when there's a storm, like last night," I finished.

Addison rose and walked down the porch, lost in her thoughts. She turned at the end and walked back. "It sounds too incredible," she said. "I want to believe it's all true."

"You think I'm lying?" I asked.

"No! Of course not, but there are stories around the village about what solitude on that island can do to someone's mind." I started to interrupt, but she began again. "Your visions, your

179

haunting experiences, explain so much about the mystery of the lighthouse and the disappearance of Caroline. The questions about what happened to her and Colin are gossip among the old-timers in the village. Those tales have mythic, unimaginable significance around here. Most believe its just good lore for tourist conversations."

She paused again, deep in thought. "Your experiences at the lighthouse," she said and turned to face the Bay, "might finally put the story to rest. We might finally know what happened." Addison moved away and stood at the railing. She struggled to stay in one place, unable to contain her excitement. "And Caroline, my Caroline. She might still be there. Oh, Daniel, I have to come visit, and soon!"

"Remember," I began, "a lot of what I encountered are nothing more than vivid dreams, nightmares."

Addison faced me. "We need to do something about those dreams, too, Daniel. Maybe Caroline holds a key for us: to fulfill my childhood dreams of knowing more about her, and your desire to come to terms with your painful past."

I rose and stood next to her. We faced the harbor. I was relieved to have shared my secret with Addison. And who better than her? She'd known about Caroline nearly her entire life. She was the person who brought the diary to me. Now we were more than friends. My story added another dimension to our relationship.

Principal Keeper

More importantly, she believed me. She was probably the only person who would have believed me since she'd grown up living in Caroline's own words.

Chapter 30

A Last Night Ashore

Vintage dress shops were her favorite haunts, and bookstores were my passion. We both enjoyed art galleries.

We lunched at a crab stand near the pier and talked about how the village had changed since the coming of spring. I told her that I'd never seen so many businesses open, and Addison said that the tourist season had not yet begun.

There was sadness in Addison's face. We were spending our last day together. I'd return to my post in the morning, and there were no immediate plans to meet again.

"I want you to visit soon," I said.

"I'd like that." Her fork picked mindlessly through her salad.

"You haven't experienced life on the rock until you've been there in a storm, stood on the tower with rain hitting your face, and lightning crackling all around you."

"Sounds lovely," she said and smiled.

"I could use an extra hand to battle the ghosts," I told her and laughed, but she didn't appreciate my humor.

"I worry about you going back," she said. "It can't be safe. There's danger out there, Daniel."

"I can handle it." I took her hand. "I've handled it so far, haven't I?"

"What you've experienced would drive a lesser man insane."

"Addison, there are dangers at the lighthouse. It's part of the job."

"Your job description didn't say anything about ghosts," she said.

I wanted to change the subject. This was not how I wanted to spend the time we had left together.

"Promise me one thing, Daniel," she began. "Promise me you'll stay out of the caves until I visit."

"Addison, I don't think …" I started to say, but she cut me off.

"Stay away from the caves, please. I think the greatest danger is down there," she softened her voice, "where tides can rise and trap you. Stay away from the caves for me, please."

I smiled and nodded. It was enough to put her mind at ease. We'd talk about other things, like plans for future dates. The dangers that lurked beneath the rock were off limits, pushed aside for another time.

Frank Pickard

We returned to the museum to rest and dress for dinner. I went to the inn to grab a tie, dress slacks and clean shirt. While Addison napped, I roamed the museum. I came to the room with images of the lighthouse, where Annie and I had our conversation. It seemed so long ago, now. I, too, missed her mother.

I was on the porch playing with the puppy when Addison rose from her nap. She watched through the screen door before coming out to join us.

"Getting to know your roommate?" she asked.

"Yes." I reached down, picked up the dog and set her in my lap. "When do you plan to open the museum?"

"Matrons from the Historical Society will be here in the morning to plan a work schedule for volunteers and docents." She sat on the steps. "I return to New York after the meeting. I left my professors in a bind when I came for mother's funeral. I'll make permanent arrangements for the future after I meet with department faculty."

"Have you considered staying in Bellwether?"

"Sure. I'm close to thesis-writing stage in my studies, and I can do that here. I had a teaching assistantship, though, and research projects. I'd hate to throw it all away when I'm close to finishing."

"I understand."

She stared toward the street and rubbed her palms together. That's what she did whenever she was troubled. I set the puppy down, walked across the porch and sat next to her on the steps.

184

Principal Keeper

"There's no pressure, no rush to make life-changing decisions," I told her.

She didn't take her eyes off the street. "I romanticized about the lighthouse for so long, and I always believed something sinister and evil was a part of its history. Your experiences confirmed it. Out there, on the island, you're at the mercy of that evil. You can't escape. Whatever's out there can harm you in the way it hurt Caroline and Colin."

I put my arm on her shoulder. "I can handle myself, don't worry. When you get back to Bellwether, come visit me. You'll see for yourself. I wouldn't have you anywhere near Seward Lighthouse if I thought it were dangerous."

The subject was closed. Our time was drawing short. We dressed for dinner and began the drive down the coast. I drove. We climbed a mountain where we could see the ocean far below. The pines were thick. There were steep turn-backs as we descended to sea level. When the road came to the water again, we were in a town much like Bellwether. At the end of the main thoroughfare, Addison told me to turn left down a side street that was no wider than an alley. At the end was a steep hill. At the top was the 'Jessica Ruth Inn'. We entered through the lobby, past the desk clerk, and then up narrow stairs to the second floor. There was a dining room with a balcony facing the ocean.

The restaurant was half-full with early diners. We were seated on the balcony. We watched the ocean grow darker, and saw the conning lights of a freighter passing on the horizon. There were votive candles and a sprig of wildflowers on the table. Paper lanterns scalloped the roofline above us. The lights grew brighter and illuminated our faces. Her eyes sparkled and she smiled. She looked young and full of life. Here was a moment on which dreams were made, I imagined.

"You have never looked more beautiful," I told her.

"The food is wonderful here," she said.

"I'm sure it is, if you think so."

"You sound like a kid with a crush," she said and laughed.

"I'm sure," I said and looked at my menu. "You look wonderful."

She glanced around the room. "This place is special to me." Addison looked at me. "And the company I'm with isn't too shabby either." She smiled. "I haven't come here often, just on festive occasions like birthdays, the prom, and graduations."

"I'm flattered you brought me here," I said.

We ordered and spoke little during our meal. We simply enjoyed each other's company. Addison caught me watching her, but she didn't seem to mind. We finished dessert and shared the last glasses from our carafe.

"What attracted you to the position of principal keeper of Seward Lighthouse?"

"I'm surprised you haven't asked me that before," I said.

Principal Keeper

"The answer wasn't important before," she said. "And now it is."

"You already know that my failed career in New York had me running away from people. I couldn't have found a more isolated place to hide," I said. "In retrospect, the job appealed to me because I like to read," I smiled. "I enjoy solitude, reading and writing."

"Writing?" she asked.

"I keep a journal. I have for years, long before my island life."

"What do you write in your journal?" she asked.

"Boring stuff. I record innocuous, mundane things: personal thoughts, meetings with harbor seals, conversations with flocks of seagulls, and an occasional original idea. It's hard to break the habit if you keep a journal. It's therapy."

"What's the difference between a journal and a diary?" she asked.

"Probably nothing," I told her.

"So, like Caroline, you keep a diary? Do you write about me, Daniel?"

"Oh, you fill chapters. I've gone through two journals since I met you," I joked. "Reams, volumes, page-after-page of stuff on …"

"Enough. Don't laugh at me," she said.

I reached across the table for her hand. "Truth is, I struggle some days to think of things to write, but when you came to the island … well, I've written a lot since."

"Can I read your journal?" she asked.

"That's not a good idea. No one has ever seen them, not even my wife. When you keep a journal, you write assuming no one will ever read it, so you're free to write anything, no matter how personal. When you share it, and you begin to write again, it's in your head that someone may read it. That inhibits you."

"So there's no hope?" she asked.

"Sorry. If I let you read my journal, I'd have to start over, new life, new friends, and new journal. It's dangerous."

"Maybe Caroline's diary has that same kind of danger, Daniel."

"I don't think so. She's gone," I told her.

"Is she really, are you sure?"

With that thought, we rose to leave. The dining room was now crowded. On the landing to the first floor, Addison and I stepped aside for two women coming up the stairs to the restaurant. When we reached the lobby, I froze, and then rushed back up.

"Daniel?" Addison called after me.

I came back down the stairs. I was certain that one of the women who passed us was the dark lady who stood at the windows the day before and who played the piano in the ballroom. But the women were nowhere in sight when I returned to the restaurant.

"Daniel?" Addison asked, "What is it?"

Principal Keeper

Addison sat next to me and rested her head on my shoulder on the drive back up the coast. I lowered my window to enjoy the cool night air and sea breezes.

"And so," I concluded, "the same woman passed us tonight on the landing. First time at the windows in Bellwether, then in my dream, in the ballroom early this morning, and again tonight."

"You're certain the note she gave you in the lobby said *Lost Souls* in Latin? I can take it to the university with me tomorrow and ask someone in the languages department to decipher it," she offered.

We drove straight to the museum. We stayed up the entire night and talked about our childhoods, likes and dislikes, favorite subjects in school, books and movies. She told me about her "silly" fear of bees and I mentioned my aversion to spiders. Neither of us cared for snakes. Addison said she liked children after meeting the family of a senior professor in her department. I talked about my son. Her favorite book was Bach's *One*, and I said my choice was Melville's *Moby Dick* because it inspired my love of reading. We both appreciated classical music and Yo-Yo Ma, and Sting's *Fields of Gold*.

Before we fell asleep, she asked what my favorite thing was about living on the island. I told her that the secluded beach was special, but I'd grown fond of the sound of the foghorn. Its voice, I explained, is an ode to sorrow, isolation and loneliness. It reminds me of bare trees in winter. When it calls out in the darkness, you feel the sadness of forever and the brevity of life. Your soul weeps, I said. It seeks no comfort, but offers solace and hope to whoever hears it. It's content to be alone. It's me.

I heard her sigh. Then she said, "Not anymore, Daniel. I'm here now."

I pulled her closer. It was a good final day.

Chapter 31

Home Again

Addison was asleep when light peeked through the curtains and spilled across the floor. I planned to slip out, unseen and unheard, and leave her a note to call when she was back from the City. I never liked 'goodbyes', and this time was particularly hard. I tried to pull my arm out from under her shoulders and ease her back onto the pillows.

"Daniel?" She struggled to open her eyes. It'd been a late evening.

"Shssss, it's okay. I need to get going." I rose from the bed.

With her eyes half open, "So soon? It isn't light, yet," her eyes closed again.

I looked at the windows and whispered, "Oh, yes, my love. It's light and my boat is at the dock."

I slipped down the stairs and taped my message to the newel post at the bottom. It read, *You were too peaceful to wake. Call me soon. Love, Daniel & Maggie.* I drew a paw print at the bottom.

I rushed over to the inn, collected my things, and checked out. Mist rose from the warm water into the cooler air. I thought I'd be late, but I arrived in time to see the launch circle the harbor and make a final approach to the pier.

I stood in the bow holding Maggie and watched the tower rise up from the water. I was anxious to see my home. I'd been away long enough. It was time to resume my duties as principal keeper.

"There's your new home, Maggie," I whispered. "I think you'll like it."

Tobias waited with his bags on the landing. He'd raised the collar of his pea coat, and the smoke from his pipe circled his stocking cap. He looked like a seasoned keeper. The water was calm, perfect for a smooth transition of two caretakers to-and-from the dock.

"Thank you again, Tobias," I called out as the boatman pushed away.

"Any time, young fella', any time," the old man called back.

I placed Maggie on the pier and she scurried clumsily up the stone steps and headed off toward the cottage.

On inspection, everything was in order, just as I'd left it. I went to the tower and surveyed the world from my center of the universe. With collar pulled up, cup in hand, I sat on the stool and leaned against the lamp house. The sun warmed the ocean. The view was more beautiful than I remembered. I understood, now, why

Principal Keeper

keepers coveted their rock assignments and stayed on for as long as time, the ministry and life would allow.

Sailboats dotted the Bay and lobster boats trolled further out. By this hour, the pier fishermen had lines in the water below the dock. Addison would be up and packing, and found my note. I can see her smiling when she saw Maggie's signature paw.

It was as though my stars were aligned. I felt no regrets for past deeds for the first time since coming to Bellwether Bay. I was looking forward, not back. The future was promising. I had a mood adjustment during my shore-side vacation. There were good days when I was young, but not so much in recent years. I'd enjoy the feeling for as long as possible.

The weather held fair. When I descended the tower and inspected the equipment, I discovered that Tobias had done an exceptional job of maintaining the facility. The brass was polished, rain gauges were cleaned, and he'd applied fresh paint to the foghorn bell housing. I avoided that task before I left on vacation.

I paused at the capstone to the caves and remembered my promise to Addison. I yearned to stand on the private beach at the mouth of the cave, but I'd wait for her.

I walked to the sea wall along the perimeter of the island to look for items that may have washed ashore. I wanted to stand on the cliffs above the cave and dream of a time when Addison and I could share the private world in the caverns below.

There was nothing out of the ordinary on my inspection, except for a large number of jellyfish that resembled a blanket of chiffon. They'd washed up with the tide and were now dying in the noonday sun. Maggie sniffed the poor creatures, and then ran ahead.

I stood on the cliff, high above the surf, a solitary figure on a precipice of stones, and surveyed my domain. I wasn't a fool. I knew that my euphoria for the island's beauty was driven by my feelings for Addison. She was part of my life now. I could conquer anything with her support, and the mysterious doings on and below the island, and in my dreams, were not a threat.

After dinner, I attached deck cord to Maggie's collar and took her to the top of the tower. She needed to be larger and more mature before I'd let her roam the balcony without a lifeline. For now, she'd wander the gallery catwalk to the length of her leash. If she slipped over the side, I'd reel her in with the cord.

I thought she might fear the height, but I was wrong. She didn't slip, either.

"You're going to make a good rock dog, aren't you?" I said as she settled beneath the legs of my stool.

Light waned, the gulls stopped buzzing the tower and squawking at Maggie, and the waves dropped to a whisper. The red lights on the buoy markers in the harbor grew brighter.

My soul was content. I took Maggie and we retired to the cottage. I built a bed for her out of old quilts, and put it in the sitting room next to the desk. She scampered after me when I started up the stairs, but she was too small to climb the steps.

"You sleep on the first floor, young lady," I told her over the banister.

She listened, and then resumed her whimpering and jumping at the stairs.

In the darkness, I heard her calm down and imagined she'd resigned to the quilts in the corner. I didn't hear a sound out of Maggie when wind rattled the shutters.

It was calm in the morning. Maggie was up and waiting at the bottom of the stairs. Her whole body wagged when she saw me come out of the bedroom.

"Looking for breakfast?" I asked. I picked her up and scratched her neck. "We have chores before we eat." I put on my stocking cap and headed out toward the tower with Maggie on my heels.

She mastered the routine by the end of the week. She grew quickly. One day she climbed the stairs in the cottage, but still slept on her quilts. She struggled with the tower steps, so I'd carry her to the top, but I dispensed with the safety line. She was too large to slip through the crossbars on the bottom of the railing. There was also a wire mesh a foot high welded to the railing that provided added protection.

I worried that she might fall on the catwalk stairs, so I carried her down when we descended. As Maggie grew, so did my biceps. It

195

was a win for both of us. I inadvertently left her behind one day and she began to howl. Her yelps echoed in the shell of the tower. I was already at the top, changing a lamp.

"In a minute," I shouted down. "Let me get this mounted first, and then I'll come get you." But her crying only grew louder.

I emerged from the trap door and started down the winding stairs. Her tail wagged in high gear. She was unapologetic about the considerable noise she'd created.

"Good grief!" I said when I reached the bottom. "You know how to get attention, don't you?"

I paused over the capstone. A quick peak wouldn't hurt. My promise to Addison was that I'd stay out of the caves, not that I wouldn't look into them.

I slid the stone aside, and Maggie and I stared down into the well. The walls and bottom were dry, as dry as I'd ever seen them. I was tempted to inspect how far the water line had fallen, but I was determined to keep my promise. My inspection would wait for another day.

My dreams were quiet. There were no storms, so I didn't anticipate any haunting from the blue lady.

Addison called in the middle of the second week. She was still in New York. She planned to be there for a few more days.

"I'll call the minute I reach the village limits," she said through the ship-to-shore radio. "Maybe I can hitch a ride out to the island."

Principal Keeper

"I'm looking forward to seeing you, Addison."

"Me, too," she answered back.

It was wonderful to hear her voice. I could wait another day or two, and I had Maggie for company. I reached down to where she sat beneath the radio table and scratched her ears.

In another week, Maggie had grown enough to follow me everywhere. She was my constant companion regardless whether I was cleaning gauges, painting the shanty, or keeping watch on the tower. We bonded. I didn't talk to myself anymore. Now, I engaged in complex conversations with Maggie, and she listened carefully to everything I said, and behaved as if she understood every word.

Addison called in the fourth week to say she was delayed, again, but hoped to be home soon. Summer was coming, and so were the seasonal storms common this time of year. Temperatures were warmer, but experts told me that weather conditions could be as severe as I'd experienced in winter.

Maggie and I woke one morning to gray skies. The clouds were high and wispy. A sinister calm fell over the ocean at mid-day, and the monitors registered a change in the direction and temperature of the wind. Barometric pressure was rising, and my call to the weather station confirmed that a front was moving in from the east.

"Don't know how big she'll be, Daniel, but it's best to anticipate the worst," the voice on the radio crackled.

"We'll be ready for it," I told him.

"We?" the voice asked.

197

I looked at the fur pile next to my chair. "This'll be Maggie's first storm," I said.

"Aye, yer mutt. I forgot. Well, both of ye keep dry, now."

"We will." I looked down at Maggie. She was listening, as usual. "Did you hear that? You and I need to make preparation for a storm."

Maggie sat up as if to say, "Okay, where do we begin."

"Come on, Maggie girl, there's work to do," I said, and moved toward the door. She rushed past me and out into the rain. She hesitated on the front stoop, and raised her nose into the air to measure the direction of the wind and the changing elements.

"You're definitely a rock dog, Maggie," I said and rushed off for the tower.

Chapter 32

A Visitor from the Past

With darkness, came the storm. It threw its full force upon the harbor and the lighthouse. Maggie was suspicious of the noise and high wind when she joined me on the tower balcony, but was unfazed, even when her fur was drenched and matted by the rain.

"We need to dry you out, girl," I said when we descended and made our way to the warmth and security of the cottage.

I used old towels to wipe her coat, then built a fire in the fireplace and pulled her quilt bed closer to the hearth. She curled up and I wrote in my journal before turning out the lamp and retiring to the bedroom.

Maggie's bark woke me an hour later. I rose and came to the landing at the top of the stairs. She stood at the front door, her head cocked to one side, as if someone were waiting.

"What's up, Maggie" She turned to look at me. "It's just the storm. Lay down, go back to bed." She trotted over to her corner.

I wasn't back in bed before I heard rumbling, like distant thunder. Then I smelled gardenia, the scent of the blue apparition. The alarm on the tower lamp blared. I came down the stairs, reset the breaker and looked out the window. The lamp was out. I ran up, dressed and came down the stairs again. Maggie met me at the bottom, eager to join in the task. We stepped outside and I looked up at the dark tower.

A deafening howl spun me around. Two harbor seals behind us, mouths open, brayed their displeasure. They were harmless, but noisy, and Maggie's presence upset them even more. I ran toward the tower, but Maggie welcomed their challenge and barked at them. I fumbled with the latch, but before I could open the door, another seal howled at my shoulder. I opened the door, stepped inside and closed it. Maggie could take care of herself, I reasoned. I didn't want a herd of harbor seals in the tower.

I put my foot on the first step and the lamp above ignited. I paused, relieved, but needed to explore why it failed. A third of the way up, the light turned downward, just as it had before, and flooded the tower room. Spider web shadows lined the walls. At eye level was the hanging corpse, only this time it was my body.

I fell backward against the wall, slid down the stairs and reached for the door, but fell. I reached for the latch and a hand grabbed my wrist. It was Colin. He grabbed my neck. I couldn't breathe. But then I sat up in bed. Maggie was curled up at my feet. It was a nightmare.

Principal Keeper

I rubbed my eyes. "So you learned to climb the stairs," I said and shook my head to clear the ugly thoughts. She thumped her tail, as though to say, "I'm here. It's okay."

Her ears twitched. She raised her head and stared at the doorway. I rose, stepped into the hall and stood at the top of the stairs. The lower room was quiet and dark, except for the sound of piano music. It was the same tune the young woman played in the ballroom at the inn. The melody was faint, but it filled the house. Then it faded away.

Chapter 33

"The launch is on it's way out, Daniel," the voice on the radio announced.

Maggie and I were outside, and came running when we heard the bell.

"What's up?" I asked.

"You've got company coming out to visit, boy."

"Inspector?" I asked.

"Nah, personal folk, a woman," the radio crackled.

"Thanks, I'll be ready."

I turned to Maggie. "Com'on. You can help tidy up before Addison arrives," I instructed.

I raced around the cottage, picked up books and papers, and washed dishes. Maggie, too, was busy. She battled with her quilt bed, and dragged it from one side of the room to the other. I snatched the binoculars from the shelf and ran to the dock. The launch was two thirds of the way out. I had just enough time to shave and change before she arrived.

Principal Keeper

I stood on the dock and watched the boat make a final turn toward the landing. I'd wait until Addison was settled before I spoke of the renewed haunting.

She was seated in the center of the boat and wore a large-brimmed straw hat that required both hands to hold it on her head. The brim hid her face. She stood and prepared to step out of the craft. I reached to help her onto the dock and realized it wasn't Addison.

"Hello, Margo," I said, as she turned back to take her handbag and briefcase from the boatman.

"Daniel," she said and smiled. "Nice little island you have here."

She walked past me to the concrete steps and looked up. "That's a big tower, isn't it?" she said. "You're not compensating for anything, are you? I know better, don't I?"

"It's been a while, M." I walked past her toward the house.

"Six years, or so, isn't it?"

The boatman hollered, "See you at six-thirty, Daniel!"

I waved to him and continued up the path. "Not staying?" I said to her.

"Not long, no," she said and followed me.

Maggie eyed Margo with suspicion, and paced her as we crossed the yard.

"It's okay, Maggie," I said and reached down to pet her. "You're out of your social circles up here, aren't you, Margo?"

203

"A little more rugged than I'm used to, yes," she conceded.

I stepped aside and she passed into the house, where she removed her hat and placed it on the kitchen table. She looked around the room. "This is rustic and homey."

"How's Peter?" I asked.

"Peter?"

"Our son, or have you abandoned him, too?"

"Oooh, getting nasty now, aren't we?" She moved past me and into the center of the sitting area. "Peter's fine. He loves his new school. He's at Ashford Academy now. Lots of friends, lots of playmates."

"Have you succeeded in your quest to erase any memory of his father?" I asked.

"Cut me some slack, Daniel. Peter knows who his father is. He thought it was fascinating when I told him you lived in a lighthouse now."

"When will you let him come to see me?" I asked.

"The courts gave me full custody, remember?"

"I know what the courts and your lawyers gave you, Margo. When, if ever, will you let me see my son?"

"It will be out of my hands soon. He's a teenager. I hear that young people his age turn rebellious toward their parents. He'll probably get fed up with me, as most people do, and go looking for your lighthouse. By that time he'll romanticize about who his father is and want to come and bond with you, I'm sure."

Principal Keeper

"What possessed you to leave the comfort of your estate and make the journey up here?"

"Jerry's dead," she said with no hint of emotion.

"Jerry Weaver?"

"Yeah, heart attack." She sat in my reading chair and began to pick lint from the armrests. She dropped invisible fibers onto the throw carpet.

"Jerry was a good man. How's his family?"

"Oh, you know Helen. She's a survivor, and the kids were either in college or had families of their own. It was a big funeral with oodles of friends and employees from the firm, then everyone went back to work."

"You could have sent a letter, Margo. You didn't need to tell me in person," I told her.

Margo rose and walked to the kitchen. She opened the refrigerator. "No Perrier, Daniel? You've slipped a long way, haven't you?"

"Get to the point of your visit."

"Jerry was head of the firm. He took over when father ... well, you know what happened to father." She walked to the bottom of the stairs and looked up. "Jerry's been dead for six weeks and the company's going backwards."

Now I understood. "It's not going to happen," I began. "I'm not interested."

205

"You respected my father and he always said you were the one who should be running the company: said you were the brightest of the bunch."

Margo now stood at the radio table, next to the library at the back of the room.

"My track record put me at odds with the share holders, remember?" I said.

She picked up the microphone on the desk. "The Governing Board sent me to talk to you," she said. There was a resigned, complacent tone in her voice.

"You're not listening, Margo."

She picked up a manual on the mechanics of weather measuring equipment and thumbed the pages. "Not a cushy job here, is it?" She dropped the book on the table and turned toward me. She came to within inches of my face, and held my stare, then reached down, took my right wrist and lifted my hand for inspection. "These don't look like the hands of a talented stock broker anymore."

"I like my job here," I told her.

"Do you? How much do you make sitting up in that tower outside? Thirties, forties, surely not more than that, Daniel." She walked away. "Let's cut the crap, shall we? The Board authorized me to offer you whatever you want to come back. You can write your own ticket, set your own salary and options scale. Choice parking, penthouse office with private garden and exercise track, it's all yours for the asking. Daddy's old office, remember?"

Principal Keeper

She looked at me. I dropped my chin and my arms hung limp. I recalled a time when Margo's offer was everything I worked for and desired. I had no doubt about my skills to run the company. An offer to take over the firm was enticing. I could avoid the foolish mistakes that ruined my career, and make amends for past deeds.

I also knew this would be the one and only offer the firm would make for me to come back. They were desperate. Margo was desperate.

"You're thinking about it, aren't you? I can tell. I know you better than anyone. You want it so bad that you can smell it," she said.

"Not anymore," I told her, my eyes still on the floor.

She sensed my hesitation. She was shrewd, calculating, and much was at risk for her if I didn't return to the firm. She'd manipulated me before, and I was certain she was confidant she could do it again.

"There's one more thing," she said. "I'll open the door to your son."

I raised my eyes and looked at her.

"You can visit him whenever you wish," she said. "There's no hope for you and me, but you can re-establish your relationship with Peter, get to know him, and let him get to know his father."

I walked past her and slumped down into my chair.

"It's an offer, as they say, that you can't refuse, Daniel."
Margo played her trump card. She was confident, I knew, that I was
seriously considering her offer.

"What do you get out of this, Margo? What's in it for you?" I
asked. "There has to be something big in it for you or you wouldn't
be here. You wouldn't travel this far to deliver a personal message
just because an aging group of tight-assed managers asked you to do
it."

"You can figure that out for yourself," she said.

"It's money, isn't it?" I said.

"Father was the major stock holder. I stand to lose if the
company folds, or drops in market value."

"And you're willing to prostitute your son to keep your
money and extravagant lifestyle?"

"I wouldn't put it like that. Peter needs to know his father.
It's in his best interests for several reasons."

"Convenient for him if I help you keep your fat bank
account, is that the way you reason it?" I asked. "Your benevolence
is admirable, Margo."

"Ashford Academy isn't cheap. You come back, Peter gets a
father, and I get the means to provide him a good life."

"Putting our son in Ashford Academy is what you consider
providing him a good life?"

"Yes, that and much more."

Margo waited for me to respond, but instead, I walked out the door. She followed as Maggie and I went straight to the tower. She struggled to walk across the rocky ground in her spiked heels. Maggie and I were halfway up the spiral stairs when Margo entered the lighthouse.

"It's how you deal with everything, isn't it? You walk away," she shouted up at me.

I looked down. "You divorced me, remember?"

Margo's heels faired no better on the honeycombed steps, but she made it to the top. I was busy pulling fuses out of the power box beneath the lamp housing. She stepped toward the balcony doorway and paused. "Is it safe to go out?" she asked. She was out of breath and wiped her face with her handkerchief.

"Sure. Watch your step, particularly in those heels."

"You're not going to throw me over the side or anything, are you?

Without waiting for an answer, she stepped out and took a firm hold of the railing. Maggie followed her and marched around the circumference of the balcony as if to say, "See it's easy."

Minutes later, I followed them onto the catwalk and assumed my post facing the harbor. The weather had cleared enough from the night before that a dozen sailboats rode the tide and took advantage of the breezes. They stayed close to shore in the chance that weather conditions turned nasty, and they'd retreat to the sanctuary of their moorings.

209

"Shit, it's beautiful up here," she said in an effort to engage me in conversation. She looked at me for a response, but my attention was focused on watching the Bay with my binoculars. It was my 'this-is-my-job' pose.

She looked over the side of the tower. "Whew, you have a major phallus thing going here." When I didn't respond she said, "Tell me something. As incredibly fantastic as this view is, doesn't it get lonely out here?" I mean, don't you miss human contact, companionship?"

Maggie snorted, as if on cue, and wagged her tail when Margo turned to look at her. "Okay, how about intelligent human conversation then, or a roll in the haystack. I recall you were pretty damn good in that ballpark. Kind'a hard to lead a social life out here, isn't it?"

Three tankers plowed for northern ports. They heaved up and down in the swells farther out.

"You don't get it, do you?" I looked at Margo. She still held fast, white knuckled, to the railing. "I miss Peter more than you'll ever understand. But I have a life now, here, on this island, in this tower. I can't go back to what I was before."

"But it wouldn't be the same. You'd have complete control of everything."

"Oh, it'd the same. I'd get caught in the never-ending scramble for higher profit margins, lower overhead outlays, corporate buy-outs, and high-pressure mergers. I don't want that life

Principal Keeper

again. I found something more fulfilling and a hell of a lot less stressful."

"You can't have changed that much," she said. "You lived and breathed mergers and profit margins, and buy-outs. It's under your skin, in your blood."

"Maybe once, but not anymore." I turned and started down out of the tower.

"Daniel!" she called. "Stop walking away from me!"

Maggie and I were at the halfway mark on the stairs when Margo started down. It took her much longer to reach the bottom. When she did, we were a hundred yards away in the direction of the cliffs on the opposite side of the island.

We reached our destination and looked back, but Margo was nowhere in sight. I needed time to think. Her visit confirmed that our divorce was a good thing. Margo was born to a life of comfort and affluence. It was natural for her to want to hang on to that lifestyle.

I laughed when I thought about Margo living at the lighthouse. "She wouldn't survive without her credit cards, hair dresser, high end boutiques and tea clubs," I told Maggie. Her tail pounded the grass, as though she understood my joke.

We sat on the ledge overlooking the ocean and watched the sailboats for a half hour. When I returned to the cottage, Margo was seated in a deck chair on the porch.

"It took a while," she said as we approached, "but I figured out how to use that radio in there," she gestured over her shoulder, "and I called for a boat."

"Launch," I corrected her.

"Whatever. It'll be here any minute."

She stood and headed down the path toward the dock. I followed.

Perhaps Margo thought I walked away because I needed time to consider her offer. She probably hoped that, given time and space to think about it, I'd come to the conclusion that she was right, and that I couldn't refuse a chance to run the agency. She was wrong.

She spoke over her shoulder as she walked. "I left papers on the table. All you have to do is fill in the blanks where it says 'salary scale' and 'benefits' and such, then sign them and send them to the Board."

"I won't change my mind, Margo. I'm not going back to that life. I might have considered it years ago, but not now."

"What in hell do you see in this place!" she shouted. When she came close to the water, Margo turned to face me. "Would it make a difference if I said that *I* wanted you to come back, that it was important to me personally?" In a tearful voice, "Good grief, Daniel, I need you, too. Did you think about that? Is that what you're waiting to hear?"

I wanted to be careful how I answered her question. I understood Margo better than anyone. She could be cold and calloused, but she had a heart, too. I'd hurt her, if I weren't careful. She was the mother of our child, and we were once married and very much in love. No, I wasn't going to say anything to purposely harm Margo.

"No, that's not what I wanted to hear. Any sane man would jump at your offer ... without the salary and stock options thrown in.

She forced a grin. "You always were a smooth talker," she said, and turned back toward the water. She walked the length of the path and down the steps to the landing. "By the way," she said as the launch approached, "they said you have another visitor coming out to see you."

I froze, looked up, and saw a woman in the approaching boat. It was still too far away to see her face, but I was certain it was Addison.

"Maybe you have reasons for staying here that I don't know about," Margo said as the launch pulled alongside the pier.

Chapter 34

New Discoveries

I extended a hand to help Addison onto the landing, and then turned and assisted Margo as she stepped into the craft.

"I hope you ..." she smiled and stared at Addison, "... and your lighthouse have a happy life together, Daniel." She waved half-heartedly, then turned and sat down as the launch heaved into the waves and made for shore.

"Margo?"

"How did you know?" I asked as we watched the boat.

"Lucky guess?" she said. "In truth, she was very vocal about who she was and her relationship with you when she arrived in the village and made arrangements for the trip out here. Villagers don't see many people like her in the offseason, and when they do, it makes for good conversation. I discovered she was coming out to see you when I stopped to pick up my mail."

We started up the steps to the path. "She made me an offer, a business proposal," I confessed.

Principal Keeper

"You don't have to tell me why she was here, Daniel."

I touched her arm. "Yes, I do. I want you to know everything, including my life before Bellwether Bay. It's a good starting point for us." I stared into her sea-green eyes. "Besides, it should flatter you that your boyfriend gets job offers from corporate giants in New York." I opened my eyes wide, "Hey, if I took their offer, we can move to New York where you can finish your studies." I said.

"Don't joke, please. Is that what you are, my boyfriend?"

I was serious, then. "I pray it's more than that." I studied her face and eyes, and then held her close. "What are you afraid of, that I'll take their offer?"

"Yes, I think you might. You should at least consider it."

"Not a chance, Addison."

"But it was your whole life, personal and professional, once."

Maggie recognized her and begged for attention. "She's grown so big!" Addison said as she leaned down to pet the excited dog.

It was too late in the day for her to return to the mainland, but she had to go back in the morning. "I arrived today and I have meetings with the cultural board to hear what arrangements they've made to staff the museum. They're expecting me tomorrow. But, we have tonight," she said and clutched my arm.

It was a new experience to have someone stay with me. But it was inevitable if we continued our relationship and I kept the keeper post. An overnight visit was a first step.

215

Addison walked the grounds and explored the facilities with interest and wonder as if it were her first visit. She paused to look at wall hangings and my book collection in the cottage. She took a piece of polished driftwood from the shelf, and ran her hand along the streaks of beige and brown.

"A treasure from the cave?" she asked.

I nodded.

She came to the bottom of the stairs and looked up. "Bedroom?" She smiled.

I shrugged my shoulders. "That's where I sleep and we can check it out together later, if you wish."

Addison asked if we could go up in the tower.

"Wouldn't you rather see the caves first?"

"I'm uncertain if I'm mentally prepared, yet," she said, and bit her lower lip.

"Better now while it's light, then when the sun sets," I told her.

It had taken years for her to arrive at this moment, I thought. Dreams were about to become reality for her. Would she be frightened, or disappointed? Addison spent her life running headlong into anything that captured her imagination, but this was different. The diary was a framework for her life. Seeing Caroline's secret world would touch the core of her childhood imagination.

She didn't speak, and I took that as a sign that she was ready to make the journey into a place she'd only imagined. We put on

Principal Keeper

swimming clothes. She scolded me playfully to wait outside the bathroom while she changed. Rocks in the caverns were sharp, so she wore water shoes, and I had a worn pair of deck shoes.

I worked the bar under the edge of the capstone and slid it to the side. Addison stepped forward to take her first look into the well. A rush of cool briny air brushed our faces. The light receded into the haze at the bottom. Maggie nosed between our legs to take a look.

I helped Addison onto the iron ladder and she inched down into the hole.

"Wait here," I commanded Maggie when she began to bark. She wasn't happy about being left behind.

At the bottom, I handed Addison a sealed-beam flashlight and we started back into the tunnels. She was quiet. Our light beams danced along the walls and over the jagged rocks in the darkness of the first cavern. Addison shined her light into several pockets in the walls, places where Caroline might have hidden her treasures. She was excited each time she discovered a new shelf, but disappointed they were all only a few inches deep. She soon realized that there were no major discoveries to be made in this first tunnel.

I knelt and swam into the second cavity, then returned to assure her that it was safe to pass through. The second, larger cave gave her renewed hope that she'd find an unexplored niche or unturned stone that hid something. She searched the walls carefully until sunlight from the mouth of the cave ahead captured her

217

attention. I was seated on the beach and staring at the water when she arrived.

"Oh, Daniel, it's wonderful! Just as she described it!" She sat next to me.

"It's difficult to explain," I said, "but I think I felt the same way Caroline did the first time I came here, as though I'd been here before, many times. Weird, right?"

We were silent, enjoying the view. Waves broke over the shallow reef and ran up onto the beach. I renewed my love for this place. I'd been away too long. Addison was thrilled by the experience. This was the place written about so lovingly in Caroline's diary, and the place of many of Addison's dreams.

The air was warm and breezy, the waves, low and gentle. Addison picked a good day to come. Margo's visit was disturbing, but now with Addison, in this place, could not have been better planned. I thought about the dinner I'd make for her. We'd spend the evening on the tower gallery watching lights in the harbor. If we were lucky, we'd have a minor rainsquall push through in the middle of the night and isolate us further from the rest of the world. Any doubt I may have had about my decision to turn down Margo's lucrative offer was gone when Addison scooted closer to me on the sand.

We spent an hour and a half watching the waves. When the tide reached our feet and the sun sank lower on the horizon, and silhouetted the hills above the village, I knew it was time to leave.

Principal Keeper

"Will Caroline's spirit visit us tonight, Daniel?" she asked as we weaved through the tunnels.

"I don't know. Perhaps. Are you convinced now that there's no treasure in these caves?" I asked.

"I haven't given up hope that there are more discoveries to be made in this lovely subterranean world," she said and took one last look before climbing up the iron rungs to the lower tower room.

I made a chunky vegetable and potato stew served with sweet bread, cheese and wine for dinner. Peach sorbet was our dessert.

Addison laughed when she'd finished her ice cream. "Do you always dine this elegantly out here?" she asked.

"Only when I have special guests over for dinner," I said.

"How often do you entertain here in your opulent surroundings?"

I mimed counting on my fingers, "Well, let's see. This year alone ..."

"This being your first year as principal keeper," she reminded me.

"Yes, but this year alone," I continued, "I've had..." I raised a finger, "...one." I smiled. "If you don't count the restless spirits."

We both laughed. "Are you making fun of my humble life here on the island?"

"Of course not," she said.

"Are you saying you wouldn't like to live in these modest conditions?"

She looked around the cottage, "This is a bit smaller than my current digs, but I think I could be happy here." She turned her eyes to mine. "If you were here with me," she said.

"Come on," I said and stood. "Time to go to the mountain."

Addison was like a child, bubbling with excitement, as we stepped out onto the catwalk.

"You're not excited about this, are you?" I asked.

"I dreamt of this moment," she began, "ever since my first visit. The caves are magical, but this view of the harbor and ocean, high above the waves, is wonderful!"

I pulled a second stool from a corner of the lamp housing where I'd placed it days ago, anticipating her visit. I sat in my usual place, rocked back and put my feet up on the railing. Addison followed my lead with her stool.

"Cushy life up here, Mr. Riggs."

"I know," I said and smiled. *Oh, how I know.*

Addison was concerned when Maggie came out onto the balcony and disappeared around to the opposite side of the lamp room. I assured her that Maggie was familiar with the dangers of the tower and was more sure-footed than either of us. Maggie returned and took her spot beneath my chair.

Addison watched Maggie get comfortable. "Rock dog," I told her. "Rock dog for sure."

Chapter 35

I went into detail about my task of watching and monitoring sea conditions and the harbor traffic. I mentioned the monolith tankers and recreation yachts, as well as the speedboats that, in fair weather, circled the island taking pictures of the tower, and the bay soundings by the coastal authority several times each year.

She was interested in everything. She asked questions, and used my binoculars to explore the view. Most of our time on the tower was spent silently enjoying the moment. Addison said that she loved the music made by the cries of the gulls as they circled above and below.

"Oh, I almost forgot," she said when the sunlight dimmed and a haze settled on the ocean. "Inspector Mason asked me to pass this on to you." She pulled a sealed letter from her coat pocket.

I tore it open and pulled out a single page letter. It was embossed with the seal of the Coastal Ministry of Lighthouse Administration. "It says that he and his guests will be coming out for the celebrations on the Fourth of July. What celebrations?" I asked her.

"That's right. This is your first year in Bellwether Bay. You don't know. Every year the ministry sponsors a picnic in Bailey Park, along the shoreline. They arrange for fireworks, launched from the deck of a barge in the Bay. Commissioners and dignitaries showoff for their friends by bringing them out here to Seward to watch the show."

"So there'll be visitors on the island for fireworks?"

"Unless it rains, yes. Mother was invited once, but I never got an invitation."

"You do this year," I told her.

"Really? You must be an important person in this community, Mr. Riggs," she joked.

"I am. Stick with me, baby," I said in my best Bogart impersonation, "and I'll take you places you never dreamed."

"Oooooh," she said in a ditzy, overly feminine voice. "I'm with you, big boy!"

✳✳✳

It was late when we fell asleep. There were no ghostly visits or haunting music. Addison was still asleep when I went to my post on the tower. She joined me with cups of coffee.

The morning breezes tossed Addison's hair. She repeatedly pulled strands off her lips so that she could drink from her cup. She was aware that I was watching her.

Principal Keeper

"There's never a bad view from up here, is there?"

"No." I looked toward the Bay. "It changes with the weather, the time of day, and the season. It has a thousand faces, each one with its own unique beauty." I looked at her. "I don't see how anyone could grow tired of this view."

"I want to visit the caves one more time before I return to the village."

"Okay," I said.

"Only this time I want to go alone."

I wanted to tell her it wasn't a good idea. I wanted to tell her what she'd told me, that there were dangers in the caves: real and supernatural. But I knew this was important to her and that she understood the dangers. Too, I wouldn't always be there to protect her.

Addison's strength was manifested in her determination and independent nature, in her all-consuming will to face, head on, any and all things that touched her life. These were qualities I found attractive and I wasn't going to discourage them.

The caves, the mysteries of the lighthouse, as well as Caroline's life and writings, were part of Addison's youth and the person she became as an adult. This was her chance to experience what Caroline felt in her hours of solitude in the caves. She'd discover for herself what inspired Caroline's soulful writings. Until now, Caroline's life was part real, and part fantasy for Addison. The

223

caves were real, and they were an incredibly important part of Caroline's history.

No, I wasn't going to hold her back from exploring the caves on her own.

"I know you don't approve of my desire to go down into the caves alone, but I want to experience what Caroline experienced: the solitude, the peace, maybe even her lost dreams of John. I want to be the first woman to go down there alone, since Caroline was there. I know it sounds silly, but it's important to me."

It's not silly, Addison. Just promise me you'll be careful."

We set a time when, if she hadn't returned to the tower room, I'd come looking for her. As she descended the ladder, she looked up into my face and joked that I should "leave the door open and the light on", she'd be home soon, she assured me.

She paused at the bottom of the well and looked up at me one more time, smiled, then set off, flashlight in hand, down the first tunnel. My mind and heart raced after her.

✳✳✳

I learned later that she navigated through the second tunnel and came to the great cavern by the beach. She switched off her light and walked the last fifty yards into the sunlight by the shore. She carefully examined all the walls as she passed, and stopped to study rock formations and a stone shelf.

Principal Keeper

She sat by the water's edge and let her mind wander to the photos of Caroline, her baby, and to particular passages in her diary. She told me that she wanted so badly to feel as Caroline felt, here in the secret garden, so many years ago. She came to the realization that her life had been very different from Caroline's. Addison never married someone she loved as deeply as Caroline loved John. Addison never had a child. She also never felt a need to marry for security and survival. She was a woman of the new millennium, fast on her way to a professional career. She was independent, self-reliant. Addison didn't need anyone to realize her dreams or to complete her destiny.

Addison said that she knew her journey to Caroline's world fulfilled a destiny she could not ignore, the map was drawn before her time. She was certain there were reasons why she was here, alone, and that her relationship with me was part of a predestined plan. There were forces greater than the bonds that pulled us together, she said, that brought us, inescapably, to the island, and that led to her sitting alone on the slip of sand at the mouth of the cavern.

What she told me next was the most troubling. Her time in the cavern grew short. She promised herself she'd return another day and search for evidence of Caroline. She took one last look at the sea, and then heard a faint, but unmistakable sound. Music came from somewhere behind her, deeper in the cavern. She left the beach, and walked back into the cave. The sound grew as she stood where the ceiling rose twenty feet above her. A glimmer of light at the base of a wall was a colored glass ball, the type used in fishing nets, identical to the ones in my house. She picked it up. Light flooded the cave the moment she held it. Colors swirled, the translucent figure of a woman knelt a few feet away from her.

It was Caroline, crying. Her face was buried in her hands. Addison came closer. Caroline rocked back and forth in her grief. Addison said the scene was so emotionally powerful that she, herself, began to cry. She touched Caroline's shoulder. She wanted to comfort her, to ease her pain and loneliness. Addison felt the weight of Caroline's deep and profound grief.

Addison said that Caroline removed her hands from her face and looked upward into a light. Her face was full of fear. Her mouth opened in a silent scream, and her eyes grew wide. Then the light on her face disappeared. Addison looked up and saw a comet falling toward them. It grew so large that its shadow blocked out the light. Then it was dark and quiet. Addison felt as though the weight of the stone was suffocating her.

She told me that she heard my voice calling her name. She tried to call back, to tell me that she was lying beneath the celestial stone, that she couldn't breathe and her life was slipping away, but all that she was able to do was whisper my name.

Then the weight lifted, she told me, and her lungs filled with cool, sweet air and she emerged from her dream. She was kneeling in the cave, and holding a glass ball. Her face was soaked in perspiration, and tears streaked down her cheeks.

She told me all of this after I found her in the cave.

I knelt beside her. "Addison! I was worried when you were late coming up. Are you alright?" I asked and helped her to her feet.

She clutched the glass ball. "Daniel, I know what happened. Caroline drowned. Here in the caves."

"Addison ..." I began.

"No, listen, it makes sense. The villagers reported that they never found her body. That's because it washed out to sea, through the mouth of the cave. Colin didn't kill her and throw her body into the ocean like everyone speculated. She drowned, here beneath the island, and the tide carried her out. I can't explain why I'm so certain, but I am. Colin, or someone, closed the lid. Maybe it was an accident." She looked around the cave. "I'm sure she was trapped down here."

We returned to the house where she relived the details of her dream. I understood then why she was so certain about how Caroline died.

The launch arrived at noon. We stood on the pier. I held her close. She was still shaken by her harrowing encounter with Caroline's tragedy. The boat circled to make a direct approach across the breakers.

Addison stepped onto the pier. "Stay out of the caves, please," she pleaded. "I don't want you to suffer Caroline's fate."

"There's too much work to do up here. I need to get this place presentable for the July Fourth revelers," I joked. She didn't smile. "You're certain you can't stay and help me."

"You know I can't. I have my own responsibilities. I'll be back." She stepped toward the launch as it bounced against the dock. She smiled. "When everyone else is picnicking in crowded Bailey Park on the Fourth, you and I will be up in the tower.

"You'll bring fried chicken and potato salad?" I asked and helped her into the boat.

"And maybe smoked salmon and lobster."

I watched her leave. I waved until I could no longer see her face. I wanted to ask if her time alone in Caroline's cave scared her off from coming back, but I was afraid of her answer. I was pleased to hear her talk about plans for July Fourth.

Her visit was too brief, but what happened to her unraveled more of the mystery. Too, I wasn't the only person now who experienced a haunting at the lighthouse.

Chapter 36

The Eye of the Storm

By the second day following the visit from Margo and Addison, I'd fallen back into a routine. Maggie was a constant reminder of Addison. She wasn't a gawky puppy any longer. We were partners, inseparable companions dedicated to the task of keeping the lighthouse in working order. I spoke to her as if she was human, and she listened attentively.

Our world was finite, but occasionally Maggie rushed off to another corner of the island. I'm certain she busied herself with chasing away the colonies of harbor seals and gulls. I never worried about her. She was close to adult canine size and strength. There was no danger for her to encounter, with the exception of the caves.

I received a call from Superintendent Mason a week before the celebration. He detailed the plans for his visit and gave me an estimate of the number of guests expected. There was little preparation to do aside from setting up a table of drinks and snacks that Mason would arrange to have delivered the day before. I was to stand ready to answer questions about the operation of the facility, to assist guests as they climbed the stairs in the tower, and to assure any weak souls that it was safe to watch fireworks from the catwalk gallery. Mason would be the official host and lecture on the history of the light. I would stand by to confirm his comments and be the authority on the complexities of modern lighthouse management.

The only names on the tentative guest list that I recognized were Mr. and Mrs. Willard, who visited during the inspection in my first months of service, the same day I met Addison. I mentioned this to her when she called to remind me that she would be visiting on the Fourth, as well.

"Mr. and Mrs. Willard?" she repeated.

"That's right," I told her.

"Well, only Mrs. Willard will be coming out to see the fireworks," she said.

"How do you know?"

"Watch," she said, "you'll see I'm right."

Addison arrived before noon and, as promised, brought a picnic lunch of fried chicken, potato salad, as well as smoked salmon. I set up a table on the balcony so we could enjoy the view while we dined.

"Too windy for you up here?" I asked when we sat down to eat.

"Not at all," she assured me. "Look way over there." She pointed. "You can see Bailey Park on the shoreline. None of those happy revelers has a view as spectacular as this."

"I'm glad you like it, Addison."

"I love it, Mr. Riggs." Her smile enhanced the view.

The launch with Mr. Mason and his nine guests arrived at sundown. I assisted the visitors to disembark and directed them to the refreshment table. I was startled to see that the last person to exit the craft was the dark woman I'd seen playing the piano, and in the restaurant. She smiled, but said nothing. She wore a sleeveless print dress, similar to the one she wore the day I saw her at the windows in the inn. Her hair was the same, over her shoulders and down her back. Her step was light she ascended the stone steps. She turned and looked at me when she reached the path.

"Daniel?" Addison was behind me. Her voice drew my attention. "What's wrong? You look like you've seen a ghost."

I looked back at the path. "It's the same young woman I met in the inn that night, the one on the stairs at the 'Jessica Ruth Inn'," I said. "She's here with Mason's group.

"Maybe we'll have a chance to find out more about her."

The nine guests milled around, sipped wine and ate cheese blocks and melon balls until Mason announced that everyone should freshen their drink and begin the journey up to the "top of the world", as he described it. The dark lady was at the tower door. When Mason made his announcement, she turned and passed into the lower room. She'd be the first person in the group to reach the top, I thought.

Addison was correct. Mr. Willard did not make the trip out.

"How'd you know?" I asked her in a private moment away from the crowd.

"You mean you haven't heard?" Her demeanor was playful. "Why, it's all over town. Seems Mrs. Willard has taken a shine to Mr. Mason, and he's grinning ear-to-ear. Just watch them and see." She turned with drink in hand toward the lighthouse. In her best southern drawl, "Why, all the respectable town folk were shocked when they heard the news, which travelled fast, even by Bellwether Bay standards of gossip spreading and rumor mongering."

When all were gathered in the tower, Mason announced that it would be another forty-five minutes before it was dark enough to start the fireworks, then called on me to give a talk on the operation of the lamp.

"Perhaps our principal keeper will tell us a little about how this wonderful light works and how it serves to protect our seafarers from harm.

As I spoke, and drew everyone's attention to the lamp, I saw Addison through the glass, leaning on the railing. She was counting the pleasure craft, cabin cruisers, sailboats and yachts scattered in the harbor. They were arranged in concentric circles surrounding the government's barge where the fireworks were to be discharged.

Principal Keeper

When I concluded my presentation, two faint-hearted souls remained in the lamp house with me, asking questions, content to watch the show through the thick glass. The rest took places at the railing facing the harbor. I encouraged the craven to step outside, and assured them it was safe, when I stopped in mid-sentence. Caroline Cheswick was staring at me through the glass. The corners where the glass panels came together were blood red from the colors in the fireworks. Her sad eyes never left mine as she moved around the catwalk toward the group. Her face blurred when she passed from one glass panel to the next. When I thought she was far enough around the tower to be seen by the others, she stopped. While still looking at me, Caroline's face morphed into the face of the young woman. One instant, it was the ghost of Caroline, and then it was the beautiful dark lady.

I rushed through the door and took the same route along the balcony where I'd seen Caroline, but when I reached the place I'd seen her last, she was gone. So was the young woman. I looked down the side of the tower, fearful that she'd slipped and fallen, but she was nowhere. I circled until I came to Mason and his guests, but the mysterious woman was not there.

Addison saw me rush from the lamp housing and along the balcony.

"Daniel, what is it?" She was at my elbow.

"Where is she?" I asked. I couldn't hide the urgency in my voice.

233

"Who?"

"The mystery woman, the girl I helped out of the boat earlier."

"I haven't seen her, Daniel. I don't even know what she looks like. Is she with Mason's group?"

"No, she's here, outside the glass." I retraced my steps to the spot where I first saw her face. "I saw her from inside the tower. Right here!"

"You must be mistaken, there's no one on this side. I didn't pass anyone walking around to meet you."

Darkness came. Rockets shot into the sky and exploded into giant starbursts and chrysanthemums. The lights illuminated the Bay.

I counted the guests. Two were in the lamp housing, seven stood at the railing and Mason made ten, but the young woman was not among them. How was the woman there one minute and gone the next? Unless, I thought, she was never there: not in the lodge, or the restaurant, or at the piano in the ballroom. I scanned the island from the tower, and ran down the stairs and into the cottage. She was gone.

Addison met me in the courtyard.

"I swear I never saw her," she said.

"Evidently nobody did, except me." I walked toward the tower. "How are our guests?"

"They're fine, lots of 'oohs' and 'ahhhs'. They're focused on the light show."

Principal Keeper

"I don't know what it is, yet," I said, "but Caroline and this woman are somehow connected to each other."

"I'll ask around in the village this week and see if anyone else saw her, or heard anything about a mysterious dark woman," she told me.

"I'm beginning to think that I'm the only one who sees her, anywhere."

Mason and his party left at ten thirty. Everyone had one more drink before their ride arrived and all expressed appreciation for my lecture and hospitality.

For appearances and convenience, Addison shared the launch back to the village. She promised to call in a day or two, and visit again within a week.

I was alone. I posted inside the lamp housing and stared at the windows where I'd seen the faces, but all I saw was the powerful light pass over the glass. Did I see the faces at all? Was I losing my mind? Ghostly forms now haunted me in the daylight, and in crowds.

I questioned everything: the haunting, the nightmares of hanging corpses, and the elusive woman who passed in and out of my life. Were these wacky manifestations of my mind? Maybe the mental shock of transitioning from one lifestyle to another caused me to hallucinate. Was I going mad? Would I be sane enough to know when I was on the edge and step back before they hauled me away in a straight jacket?

Addison called the following afternoon to report that a meeting of the Museum Guild was planned for Saturday night, and she'd make inquiries.

"How would you like to go sailing?" she asked, and changed the subject.

"I don't know. I've never been sailing."

"Check with your bosses and see if they'll give you a few hours on Thursday and I'll pick you up."

The weather held fair for the next two days. I had time to polish brass, clean and replace worn parts and seals on the weather gauges, and apply a coat of paint to the trim on the house. The tower was due for a major repainting, but a professional crew would come out in August to complete the monumental task.

I'd never lived near the ocean, but I learned how corrosive sea air was to metal surfaces and painted structures. The brine and incessant wind took a toll on me, as well. My hair was lighter in the harsh summer sun, and it maintained a perpetual state of shock. My skin was darker and more like the texture of leather. My hands were stained by the brass polish, and calloused, and aged by the industrial strength solvents.

I studied my features in the mirror. My appearance had changed. The Wall Street executive was now the Marlboro man. I was joined to the sea and the rock, rugged to the spirit of the country and the job. I looked the part of a rock-island lighthouse keeper,

Principal Keeper

weathered and worn, but robust and powerful, and in the prime of my life.

One day I took the legal papers Margo brought to the island, and that I'd left on the desk, and threw them away. There was no going back. I was certain the offer would never be extended again. I was relieved to know that the door to my former life was shut for good. I missed my son terribly, but I was resigned to live with the hope that someday Peter would look for me and we'd renew our relationship.

Chapter 37

On Thursday, I watched from the tower as her sailboat approached. It circled and drifted toward the dock. I flew down the stairs and trotted down the path to the dock. By then the sails were dropped and the boat approached under inboard motor power. Addison stood at the wheel and called out for me to catch the bow to keep it from striking the rocks.

"How about a lift, sailor?" she called.

"Nice sailboat," was all I thought to say.

"Push off and jump."

I did as instructed, and the inboard engines reversed and backed the craft out into open water. I short-stepped back to where Addison stood at the helm in the cockpit deck. She expertly spun the chrome wheel to guide us backward across the breakers.

Maggie ran back and forth on the dock, and barked wildly.

"You're in charge while I'm away," I shouted to her. "Keep everything running smoothly."

"Time to hoist the mainsail," Addison said.

"Who's sailing this boat?" I joked.

Principal Keeper

"I am, but it'd be easier if you helped," she said, and kissed me.

I pulled one line, then another, as Addison shouted instructions. She asked me to take the wheel while she pulled a foresail from below and ran it up the jib stay. Then she checked the halyard lines. My vocabulary was expanding with each new task.

Soon we were cutting through the harbor waters, passing fishing boats and other craft. She showed me how to keep the sails trimmed to the wind, and then she sat on the bench along the well coaming as I steered.

"When did you learn to sail?" I asked in a quiet moment.

"It was a gift from my mother on my sixteenth birthday. A friend took me out on his boat a few times and I loved it, so she decided I should learn to sail."

"Where did you get this huge boat?"

"It's called a 'Vanguard three-quarter-ton sloop'. My friend rents sailboats. I got it cheap, because he doesn't rent this one often. It's too big for the amateur sailor."

"I'm impressed," I told her.

An hour later, Addison lowered the sails, dropped anchor and went below. She returned with a pasta salad, crab and shrimp finger sandwiches, and an ice bucket with four chilled beers. She set up a table in the cockpit and we sat down to eat.

"Do you think I'm losing my mind?" I asked as I opened beers and set the table with dishes she'd brought up from below deck.

"No. However I do think your presence as the principal keeper awakened restless spirits." We clicked bottles and began to eat. "It was fun cooking again," she said.

"You don't cook in the City?" I asked.

"Not often. You don't need to cook in New York City. As you know, there are a slew of restaurants. Friends and I eat out a lot. I have my favorite places, and chefs. I love the atmosphere of a quaint spot hidden on a side street, a place where locals go and keep secret from tourists. It wasn't fun cooking for just myself when I left Bellwether Bay and moved to the City."

"You didn't cook for your short-term husband?"

"No," she said, "of course not. We lived on love and Hostess snowballs. We were too busy going to rallies, attending esoteric lectures by pseudo-intellectual economists extolling the virtues of moderate consumption and the evils of the cosmetic industry that was wreaking havoc on the environment. We went to bookstores and ate lots of fruit, no meat, and used cooking oil for sexual experimentation."

"So you cook *and* sail. You're going to make someone the perfect housewife," I joked.

"Funny, Riggs. You buy and sell stocks, and manage investment portfolios, *and* you keep a lighthouse," she joked back.

Principal Keeper

I'd never studied the harbor or the village from the middle of the Bay. It was enchanting. My island was far in the distance, but its white tower sparkled in the sunlight.

"So where do we go from here?" she asked. "You and I."

"In our relationship?"

"No, silly." She leaned across the deck cushions and we kissed. "I think I know where our relationship is going. I mean the search to solve the mystery of the lighthouse."

"Well, with the arrival of the dark woman, and my sighting of her in the village, I guess the mystery extends beyond the rock."

"I still think your lighthouse holds the key to everything."

"I think you're correct." I looked back at the tower. "I think *we*," I emphasized the word and winked, "should find out what happened to Emily Mackenzie, the baby."

"I agree, Daniel."

"She could hold clues to this story. In fact, she may be the only piece we have left to complete the puzzle. Silas said he heard she was put in an institution in upstate New York, or on Long Island."

"That's something I can check when I go south."

"You're going south?" I asked.

"Yes. I have unfinished business. I need to vacate or sublet my apartment, set up a thesis schedule with my professors and check in with the graduate school. I'm determined to finish the degree."

"I think you should," I told her, and meant it.

Chapter 38

I once tried to seduce my wife on our balcony, high above Central Park, but she wasn't interested. Making love in the outdoors was a new experience for me. The mast was a sundial that registered the passing of time. Its shadow drifted as the anchored boat turned with the current.

"Daniel," she whispered. "Why do you think the spirit of Caroline visits you out there?"

"I don't know. Wish I did."

"Maybe ... maybe it's because she can't rest until we find the truth, or she finds her child. Something about you brought her spirit out of the caves."

"You've been watching the Sci-Fi channel, haven't you?" I joked.

Serious now. "If spirits haunt a place, it means their souls didn't move on when they died. Powerful emotions at the moment of death linger to haunt the living. I think Caroline was in pain when she died. There was something she needed to do and couldn't, so

Principal Keeper

now her spirit is restless. Discover what she's looking for, and we can give her peace."

I felt bad for mocking her. She made me realize that I'd only considered my own disquieted mind, and that Caroline was the haunted soul forever imprisoned on the island. But she died so long ago, before I was born. Why was I the catalyst that brought her out of the shadows? Why me? I'd been reactionary, and concerned about myself. I didn't stop to consider that I might have sparked the events.

We remained anchored in the harbor another hour, then raised the sails and turned the bow toward Seward Lighthouse.

"Let's make a sweep of the rock, what'a'ya say?" she offered. "I bet you've never seen it like the tourists do."

It was magnificent! I stood on the foredeck and shielded my eyes. The island from this view was more mysterious. The rock and tower were like a ship in the middle of the ocean. We drifted around it. I saw the gallery and the glass jewel at the top, and thought about the thousands of hours I'd spent there, and how my earliest memories of Addison were of her as she stood at the railing.

When we passed the western side, I looked for the cavern and the strip of sand. I knew exactly where it was, could pinpoint its location along the cliffs, but I didn't see it. There was no visible breach in the rocks to expose it. The secret was safe, and had been for a lifetime. High swells and the shallow reef kept us from getting closer.

243

I knew Addison couldn't stay. There wasn't a way to safely lash the boat to the dock. We could anchor offshore, but it was too dangerous to swim to the island. A single wave could render the strongest swimmer unconscious, if it threw them against the rocks.

We said goodbye quickly, so that she could reverse the engines and pull away before the fiberglass hull was damaged against the stone pier. I stood on the dock and waved until Addison turned toward the mainland.

It was then that I saw Maggie waiting, just where we'd left her hours before. She rushed up and the two of us sprinted for the point above the cliffs so that I could wave again as her sailboat passed, but she was too far away. We sat and watched the sun sink lower. When the air turned dusky orange, we set off for the cottage and tower.

I was in a playful mood, so I inventoried the contents of the emergency trunk. Theoretically, in a dire emergency, if I had to escape the island, the trunk contained an inflatable three-man raft, so the ghosts could go with me, dry-packed provisions, canned water and other survival supplies. In reality, if a hurricane swept across my island, and destroyed everything, the three-man raft would be useless.

I decided to test the automatic inflation mechanism, so I placed the package in the middle of the room and pulled the release valve. Nothing happened at first, and then there was a high-pitched

Principal Keeper

squeal as air rushed into the rubber raft. Maggie jumped and yelped, and ran for the door. I nearly did the same thing.

It took seconds. I climbed in and Maggie watched from the doorway. I explored the contents of the zippered pockets stocked with waterproof matches, flares, fishing line and hooks. I wondered when I would need the waterproof matches while I floated in the middle of the ocean.

I'd report to the ministry supply officers that the rubber craft accidently inflated itself, somehow, so they'd send me another for the emergency trunk. I coaxed Maggie back into the room, but couldn't persuade her to get into the raft with me. She sat on the floor and rested her chin on the frame like it was a rubber pillow.

I felt silly sitting in a boat in the middle of the room, but it was a good exercise. I familiarized myself with the content of the trunk and felt better prepared to deploy the emergency equipment if needed, but I doubted that I ever would. I couldn't imagine that the rubber raft would fair well in the angry seas.

I stood the boat vertically in a corner the room and prepared supper. After we'd eaten, and with a fresh cup of tea, man and dog took their positions on the tower. Three sister tankers were scheduled to pass late in the evening, going south to Boston. Heavy rain was predicted to last for an hour or so, so I monitored the traffic as it passed.

The rain started after midnight and continued until three o'clock in the morning. At morning light, a thick fog rolled into the harbor. The wail of the foghorn continued throughout the day and into the following evening. I was reading when Addison called.

"The Museum Guild met this evening." She was out of breath, and animated. "I spoke to Mrs. Tilley. Her father, Jacob, was on the crew that investigated the tragedy the night Caroline disappeared and Colin hung himself."

"Did she have any information on the baby?"

"I got the name of a foster home on Long Island." The radio crackled. "I'm going to do a computer search and check it out over the weekend. I'll keep you posted."

"Thanks, Addison."

"You owe me, Riggs."

"Care to come out tonight and collect." I laughed.

"Boy, wish I could, but I'll send you a bill and collect on it later."

"Don't take too long. Thanks for yesterday. It was nice."

"Yes, it was," she agreed. "Hang in there, Daniel. I'll be back soon enough."

With that, she was gone. I reached down next to the chair and scratched Maggie's neck. She'd been asleep and, at first, resented the interruption, but then rolled over for me to scratch her tummy.

So the journey of discovery would continue, and Addison was a major player with me in the effort. I cherished my time alone, but feelings of loneliness were deeper when Addison and I were apart. I felt close to her when I stood on the tower, because it was a

Principal Keeper

place she loved. Maggie, too, was a constant reminder, because we'd chosen her together.

Chapter 39

The Storm

It began with an early-morning drizzle that grew into a storm. Gale force wind lashed the stone structures, and surf pounded the shore. The sky was dark and ominous. Faint sunlight the following morning failed to burn through the rain clouds as they billowed and stretched from one horizon to the other. The signs were there. A major blow was coming.

"Won't be any rest this evenin', Daniel. Going to get worse 'afor it gets better," the harbormaster reported before total darkness descended on the island.

"Any traffic?" I asked.

"Nah, shippin' lanes are quiet out there t'night, but there's always a chance an inexperienced, rookie private-boat captain will try to weather the storm and come on through. All you need to worry about is staying dry and keeping the light lit."

"No problem. Maggie and I have it covered."

Principal Keeper

I signed off, finished my evening meal and went to the tower. I paused over the stone cap to the well and thought about my promise to Addison. Besides, it wasn't wise to go into the caves during a storm.

The rain was still gentle enough for me to see the lighted buoy markers in the harbor. Their red beacons blinked as they bobbed to the top of a wave crest, then fell back into a trough.

Conditions worsened by morning. The air was so charged that the radio signal from the harbor authorities was weak.

"Gettin' dicey out there, Daniel," said the voice on the radio. "Meter readings are off the scales."

"How bad do the weather experts say it's going to be?" I asked.

"Maybe the worst storm we've had in a decade, they say, hurricane winds, heavy rain and high tides. We might need to evacuate villagers who live in the low lands. That's how bad they tell us it might be."

"Okay, I'll be prepared. Thanks for the warning."

I could sense the strength of the storm with each passing hour. Soon, I'd be forced to use the guideline to get from the tower to the cottage. I might also need to stay secured in the cottage for my own safety.

Maggie, too, was nervous. She stayed close to my heels. I changed the fuses in the foghorn shanty and took an extra lamp up into the tower. I recorded measurements on the gauges before cleaning and preparing them for the next go around.

Occasionally I glanced at the meters and was astonished how high the barometers and scopes rose.

I welcomed the challenge, just as I had when I faced my first major storm, but I had no way of knowing if I were prepared for what I'd encounter this time. I had to trust that my experience would be enough. This storm would be a benchmark, a tidewater line for my evolution into a seasoned keeper. Would I pass or fail the test? I reminded myself that my predecessors faced similar storms and prevailed. If they could do it, then I could as well.

The last call from the harbormaster and weather station came in at nine forty-five in the evening.

"They're now …" and the radio crackled silent, "… going to be in excess of one hundred and …" and the signal was lost again.

"Say again, you're breaking up."

"Winds could get as high … one hundred and forty knots, Daniel, and they say that …" The voice was there, but the words were garbled. Someone was talking, but I only received every third or fourth word.

"Can you repeat? I'm not getting the message."

The line cleared, and I heard him say, "They're moving us inland, this storm's coming through like a freight train." The radio fell silent.

"You mean it's not full strength yet?" I asked.

Principal Keeper

"Nah, still gettin' stronger. Sorry we didn't see it coming sooner or we would have pulled you off, Daniel."

"Don't worry about me." It struck me that my words would be a perfect last quote for the newspapers to print when they couldn't find my body. I was impressed with my false bravado. "We'll make it through this alright!" I looked down at Maggie.

"Not sure when we'll be able to get back to you. Maybe in the morning."

"I'll be here, me and Maggie. Take care of yourself," I said into the radio.

"We're all thinking and praying for yer' out there, Daniel."

"I appreciate that …," but my words were cut short by the radio.

"Wha'd say?" the voice asked.

"I said that …," but I was interrupted again.

"Sorry, Daniel, we're losing ya'. Keep the hatches tight and we'll look for ya' at first light. Everyone here at the station …" and the voice was gone in a sea of electrical pops and static.

I signed off, not knowing whether they heard me. The rafters above me groaned and creaked. We were alone now, cut off even from radio contact with the mainland. This was total isolation.

I thought about Addison. Where was she at this moment and did she know about the danger growing in my corner of the world? Would she worry? Was she safe? What were the chances I'd never see her again? I pictured her face the last time I saw her. It was when

251

we went sailing and I pushed the boat back from the dock, and she turned for shore. She smiled and waved from her place at the wheel. She was distracted with sailing the boat. She probably didn't see Maggie and me on the cliffs as she sailed away.

Now, flashes of lightning flooded the lamp windows. I thought I'd seen the worst, but the storms I'd experienced were preludes to what I'd face before this night was over.

Chapter 40

Addison's Discoveries

Hundreds of miles away, Addison made discoveries that altered the fabric of our journey. She found the foster home on Long Island and drove over from Manhattan on Saturday morning. No directories listed the place Helen Tilley gave her. City hall was closed for the weekend, so she didn't have access to public records. She went to the one place in town that would have information, the local historical museum.

We knew that it was April 9, 1935, when villagers in Bellwether Bay made the gruesome discovery of Colin Cheswick hanging in the tower, so we reasoned that was close to the date Emily Mackenzie was brought to the foster home in upstate New York. There was a chance the records in the museum would give Addison clues where to find Emily.

The town's archival repository was smaller than the Bellwether Bay museum. It was a single-story masonry building constructed in the 1940's. There were none of the period furniture so abundant in her mother's museum. Meat-market style display cases contained tintypes and daguerreotypes, inventory ledgers, and personal artifacts such as pocket watches with embroidered fobs, clay pipes and eyeglasses worn by members of the pioneer families who settled the town. There were photographs of uniformed soldiers from every period beginning with the Revolutionary War. There were medals and award certificates, and dozens of documents that chronicled the early history of the community.

Addison reported to me later that she roamed the museum for an hour before a woman arrived and sat at a table with brochures and a donation box near the front door.

"I'm sorry," the woman said and rose from her seat when she saw Addison. "I didn't know anyone was here. I live two doors down, and I ran home to check on my husband. He hasn't been well."

While she spoke, the woman never stopped moving. She shuffled and restacked the brochures. She had them perfectly aligned but kept turning them as if the literature was never quite right. Throughout their conversation the woman's hands were busy as they moved from one cabinet or display to another. She polished tabletops, rearranged items in their cases, and touched everything in reach.

She wore a blue cotton dress with red buttons up the front. Red stitching lined the cuts and corners of her garment. It reminded

Principal Keeper

Addison of the institutional uniforms that women inmates wore at a correctional facility where she once taught a college course.

"Anything in particular that I can show you?" the woman asked Addison.

"I'm visiting for the day and I'm looking for a particular home in your town."

"Whose home was it?" the curator asked.

"I'm not certain," Addison told her, "but I think it was a foster home for children, operated in the 1930's. It was called 'Bastian House for Orphans'.

"Can't say I've heard of that one. 'Course I only moved here in the sixties when I met my husband. Neither of us was in our prime. We met late and married even later." Her laugh reminded Addison of the sound made by a particular bird at the Bronx Zoo.

Addison was anxious to get back on topic. "Could you direct me to someone who might have lived here in the thirties, or would know the history of the town at that time?"

"Well, my Clarence lived here all his life, except for a short time spent in a mill in Macon, Georgia. Clarence Milton Collier the Third. Third born, third generation, all from here, they did." As she spoke, she stacked and restacked antique hand-painted postcards with pictures of women with thin waists and bustled dresses.

"Could I speak to Clarence, Mrs. Collier?"

"Well, I don't know. He ain't been well." She stopped stacking and put her hands in her skirt pockets. "Then again, he

255

doesn't get out much, which makes him sad." She smiled. "Maybe it'd do him a world-o'-good to visit a spell with a pretty girl like you … if we make it brief."

"It won't take long for me to ask him a couple questions."

"Well, come on, then." She walked out the door with Addison close behind.

Their home was a shotgun style, a single hallway from the front door to the back, and rooms to the left and right. Homes on either side were the same, white siding, dormer attics and stoops for front porches.

Clarence was upright in his orthopedic bed. He was lanky and ashen, with shadows around his eyes. His hands were folded across his chest. Addison wondered if he was still alive.

There was a child's carousel lamp next to his bed with galloping horses. Butcher paper covered the window, so that the light was perpetually dim. Addison could smell his stale breath.

"CC?" the woman whispered and touched his shoulder. "CC, you have a visitor."

His translucent eyelids fluttered open and he struggled to focus.

"CC, honey, you got a young lady here that'd like to talk to you. I got to get back to the museum," she said to Addison. "Just poke your head in when you're done."

Addison assured her she'd let her know when she was leaving.

256

Principal Keeper

The old woman walked out of the room and pulled the door nearly shut. Addison was alone with Clarence.

"Mr. Collier?" she said.

His face contorted into a pained expression as though he were both annoyed and frightened by her voice. His eyes searched the ceiling, and then lowered and came to rest on Addison's face. His expression softened, and he smiled.

"Hello there," he whispered.

"Hi," she said. "Mr. Collier, my name is Addison, and I'd like to ask you a couple questions. Do you mind?" She leaned closer.

He pondered her question, and then said, "What would you like to know?"

"Thank you." She leaned closer. "Do you recall a place called Bastian House?

His eyes searched the room and came to rest on a half-filled glass of water with a bent straw on the table by his bed. His stare didn't waver from the glass.

"Would you like some water?" she asked, then picked up the glass and placed the straw between his lips. He closed his eyes and drank several large gulps. Addison placed the glass on the table. She waited.

Then Clarence spoke again. "Orphanage for homeless children."

"That's right," Addison said. "What do you know about it?"

257

She waited until his eyes opened again and he looked at her. "Miss Paradise," he said and closed his eyes.

"Mr. Collier, who's Miss Paradise?" she asked. "Mr. Collier?" she said louder and leaned closer to his face.

A crash of thunder shook the foundation of the house and the carousel lamp went out. The room was dark except for a sliver of light from the hallway. Addison exited the room, went down the hallway to the front of the house and pushed open the screen door. The old woman met her in the front yard.

"Boy, that was something, wasn't it?" the woman said and looked up at the sky. "Weather lady said we might get rain this afternoon, but I didn't expect it to come on so quickly." She looked at the doorway over Addison's shoulder. "How was your visit with CC?"

"I think he fell asleep."

"Yeah, he does that a lot. I'm sure he's okay. Did you find out anything?" she asked.

"No, unless the name Miss Paradise means something to you," Addison told her.

"Natty Morgan's her real name, old timers call her 'Miss Paradise'." She glanced around and moved in close to Addison. "Want to know why?" She grinned. "It's 'cause she made her living as a hooker when she came to town. She was only nineteen, but they say she was something special to look at, for sure."

"When was that, when she came to town?"

Principal Keeper

"I'm not sure exactly, but it was when CC was a young man himself. Long time ago, that's for certain."

"Is Natty Morgan still living?" Addison asked.

"Everyone knows Miss Paradise! Sure she's still living. I don't think she's ever going to die, she's so well preserved, if you get my meaning."

"Where can I find her?"

"Natty ain't going to be able to help you none, young lady."

"Why not?" Addison asked.

The old woman's voice dropped an octave. "Because she was a lowlife, nobody except the young men gave her much attention, probably didn't have any friends, I'd imagine."

"I'd still like to talk to her," Addison insisted.

Rain began to fall. Both women became uncomfortable.

"Weather service said this might turn into a major blow," the woman said.

Addison grew impatient. "Natty Morgan!"

"She lives on Chestnut, corner of Chestnut and Holly. Cream colored house with a large front porch, blue trim." She pointed down the street. "Down that way about seven blocks."

"Thank you," Addison called out over her shoulder, raised her collar and ran to her car.

259

Chapter 41

The Demon Approaches

Addison's storm in New York was a whisper compared to the fury that raged outside my door. I knew there'd be times when my lighthouse duty would be perilous. I couldn't afford to stay too long in the safety of the cottage. Among other tasks, I needed to check on the door seals and locks on the lamp room, tower, foghorn shanty and tool sheds.

Dressed for battle, I gave Maggie a stern command to wait in the dryness of the cottage, and then I headed for the tower. I labored hand-over-hand along the guideline to the metal door, stepped into the calm inside the lower room and closed the door. I took the steps in twos. It felt as though the walls and spiral stairs swayed from the hurricane-force winds. Rain came from all directions. Sheets of water covered the windows. The lamp house was a fish bowl inside a wind tunnel. I had no doubt the thick panes would hold, but it was still unsettling to be so high up in the mouth of the storm.

Principal Keeper

I checked to make certain the pressure vents in the top of the tower were open, and then went down the stairs. Halfway to the bottom, the general power failed and light bulbs went out. It was dark, except for lightning coming through the portals. I looked up and saw the lamp was still burning. Points of light, like stars, peeked through the holes in the floor of the lamp room. The lamp operated on a power line independent of the general lighting. So a breaker blew in the electrical box, but not in the grid beneath the lamp. The tower light also had a backup generator that activated automatically in a complete power failure. I'd manage without general lighting as long as the lamp continued to burn and the foghorn bellowed.

It took all my strength to hold fast to the guideline. My life would be in danger if the line broke or I lost my grip.

Wind, thunder, and the wail of the foghorn were a crescendo of noise reminiscent of my nightmare with the giant Poseidon. The sound was deafening and the elements tore at my clothes. The storm threatened to destroy everything, including me. I fell into the dark cottage and closed the door. Maggie greeted me enthusiastically in the shadows.

"It's okay, girl," I assured her. "We just have to stay low until it passes." I looked up to the ceiling, "Whenever that might be."

Candlelight illuminated the room, as the storm grew more intense. Their flames twitched like cattails. I sat in the recliner with my arm over the side, so that I could scratch Maggie's head.

We waited.

Chapter 42

Natty Morgan

Rain was still falling when Addison found the home at the corner of Chestnut and Holly. She grabbed an umbrella, got out of the car and ran up onto the wrap-around porch for shelter. She rang the doorbell. A friendly face appeared at the screened door. She was six inches shorter than Addison, with wavy gray hair, and she wore a knee-length flower-print shift dress. The tiny woman was youthful, for her years, Addison thought.

"Natty Morgan?"

"Yes, can I help you?" Before Addison could answer, the screen door opened and the woman stepped out onto the porch. "Good, grief, child! You're going to get soaked to the bone out here, then catch pneumonia, and then die." She laughed. "Never had anyone die on my porch. You don't want to be the first. Come in, come in and warm yourself."

Addison followed her though the doorway.

"Set yourself down in the front room there and take off that wet jacket," she said and walked away. "Can't be anything so important you'd risk catching your death, out on a day like today. Good golly, gracious," and she laughed again.

Natty returned with a towel and handed it to Addison, then sat in a recliner across from her and waited. Addison dabbed at her hair and clothes.

"There's water heating on the stove. We'll have tea in no time," Natty said and rocked back in her chair.

Addison looked around the room. Flower prints were everywhere, on the furniture and walls. There were foot-high oak floorboards, and lace curtains. It was colorful, warm and inviting.

"You have a lovely home, and I apologize for barging in like this."

"Thank you, and I invited you in," she smiled.

Natty's smile was infectious and unwavering. She had a lively spirit. Addison liked her right away.

"Oops, there's the pot screaming for me to come pick him up. Make yourself comfy and I'll be back in a moment."

Natty was hospitable and kind. Addison wondered if the older woman routinely invited strangers into her home?

Addison stood and walked around the room. There was a baby grand piano in the bay window. The top was covered with framed photographs, many of Natty at different ages. She was beautiful in her youth. Her hair was long and wavy, and she always

263

wore flower prints. The remaining photographs were of young girls of varying ages. She was still looking at the photographs when Natty returned with a tray.

"I call it my vanity piano," she said.

Addison picked up an early photograph of Natty. "You're beautiful," she said.

"Once, yes, but now I'm ..." she lowered her voice and pulled the word out, as if to mimic someone's observation, "... h-a-n-d-s-o-m-e." She poured the tea.

"I think you're still beautiful," Addison said.

"I apologize," Natty pointed to the photographs, "for all the photographs of me, but I didn't have any family of my own."

"But there are so many children pictured here."

"None from my loins. Didn't have time to raise my own. I have a sister, but we parted ways long ago. I have a photograph of her. You can see it there. Now, she was a looker, for sure. Tried to convinced her to go into business with me." She laughed louder than ever. "Could have made a fortune on that face and figure."

"What business was that?" Addison asked.

"Oh, come now." She put a hand on her hip, accentuating her figure. "Whoever directed you to my home surely told you how I made a living. I don't mind, really. Why, I'm an institution in this community, a walking, breathing museum artifact of the early history of this town, a fixture for the tourist traffic. Everyone round town knows the history of the infamous 'Miss Paradise!"

Principal Keeper

Addison laughed hard. "You're correct. The person who gave me directions here did say you had a shady past."

"Ooooh, you say that so nice. I like that, 'shady past'. And who was it sent you my way?"

"She's the museum curator," Addison told her.

"Ah, yes, Mrs. Collier. She'd be someone who would know my past, considering it's her job to keep an eye on all the town's museum pieces." The infectious laugh came spilling from her again. "CC? Now there's a good and gentle man, but I hear he's barely alive these days."

"Ms. Morgan …" Addison began.

"Natty, please," she corrected her.

"Natty," she began again, "I'm looking for someone who might have lived here a long time ago."

"What's the person's name, honey?"

"Emily Mackenzie or Emily Cheswick?" The look on the old woman's face was enough for Addison. "Do you know where I can find her? It's very important."

"Is it?" Natty asked and poured more tea.

"Yes. See, I live in a small town in Maine where Emily lived when she was a child. And, I understand that she was brought here after her parents died."

"Your information is correct, Addison."

265

Addison was shocked. She hadn't told Natty her name. "How do you know my name?" Addison was frightened for the first time since walking into Natty's home.

"Don't be alarmed. The answer is simple. Well, maybe not that simple." Natty rose and walked to the piano. "Did I tell you that this piano isn't just decoration? I can play it, quite well, too," she said, as though changing the subject.

"I'm sure you do, Natty," Addison said, "but I'd rather hear what you know about Emily, and how you knew my name, before you play the piano."

There was a power failure, then, and the lights went out, so the only illumination came from rain-shrouded light passing through lace.

"That happens a lot in these old homes, especially when we have a storm. I'll grab a couple candles before it gets too dark. Power could be out for a while." She left the room, and returned with the candles and matches. Natty placed one on the piano. She then sat and began to play.

"Do you recognize this tune?"

"Should I?" Addison asked, but it was familiar. She'd heard the melody during her dream in the chambers beneath the tower.

"This little tune is key to unlocking the mystery of Emily and her family." Natty played the melody again, and then closed the lid. "Emily hummed that song from the first day I brought her home, so I taught her to play it on the piano. Don't know when she first heard it." She stared at the windows, lost in her own memories.

"Please tell me about her."

"Better yet, I'll take you to her." She looked out the window. "I think it will get worse before it gets better, so we best go quickly."

Chapter 43

Natty changed into heavier clothes, and then donned a raincoat and rubber boots. She loaned Addison a knee-length coat and they went to her car. Natty directed Addison across town. Addison's mind raced to think of questions to ask Emily: Did she know that her mother kept a diary, what does she remember about her mother, does she remember anything about the night her mother disappeared?

They turned up a graveled road and passed through an arch of tall cypress. The wipers worked overtime. Addison pulled up to a metal gate. Ironwork above the arch read *Brockmoore Cemetery*.

"What is this?" Addison asked.

Natty pointed. "Up there, see that white marble building? That's where Emily is, or at least her body. Only God knows where her soul rests," she looked at Addison, "if it rests at all." The serious tone in Natty's voice frightened Addison. It was in stark contrast to the lighthearted personality she'd seen earlier.

"Come on, I have a key." Natty stepped from the car, opened the gate and walked up the path between the rows of headstones. Addison followed.

Principal Keeper

The mausoleum was open and Natty had disappeared when Addison reached the door. She walked into the chamber. Her eyes adjusted to the light from a sconce on the wall. She heard Natty's voice. The woman stood at the head of a stone coffin in the middle of the room.

"I paid extra to run electricity in here. Had to weave the wire around those graves to get it up the hill, but I wanted it that way." She slapped the surface of the marble. "Had the money, hell, I would'a spent twice as much to give her the best."

Addison felt dizzy from the shock of learning Emily was dead. Her efforts to solve the mystery shuttered to a stop in this cemetery, in a sea of graves. "How'd she die, Natty?"

"Jealous boyfriend, can you believe that? So much life, so much love to give and one idiot with an abundance of testosterone decides that he can't live without her, and she *shouldn't* live without him." She rested her cheek the surface of the casket. "I loved her so much and she had a gift."

"What kind of gift?" Addison asked.

Natty raised her head and stared at her. "You mean, you don't know?"

"Know what?"

"About her gift, of sight. Emily could see things, things other people couldn't. She knew when things were going to happen before they did. I think she knew Stewie was going to kill her, too."

"Stewie?" Addison asked.

269

"Yeah. That was her boyfriend's name. Stewart Nathan Adler, a kid from one of the well-to-do families in town. She ran off to New York City to get away from him, but he found her."

"How did he kill her, Natty?"

"Stewie waited until she got off work one day and ran her down with his daddy's Cadillac when she was crossing the street."

"How did you meet Emily?" Addison asked.

"I found her in the foster home not long after she got there."

"Bastian House," Addison said.

"That's right, but kids can be cruel and they called it 'Bastard House'." She stared off into her own thoughts as she spoke. "I saw something in that child right off, a spark, a bright light that reached out and took hold of me when I walked by that home. Emily was in the yard playing with the other orphans. She stopped and came to the gate. I'd never walked down that street before, but something inside me that day told me I should. Emily didn't talk then, but she reached her little arms up to me. You might say she chose me. I think she could sense we were both social outcasts."

The old woman's face glowed as she smiled and stared off into a dark corner of the room. They were silent.

"Natty?" Addison said.

"Yeah, sorry I drifted away," she said. "First time I saw her is special to me."

"You adopted her?" Addison asked.

"Not right off, although I wanted to, because I couldn't have kids of my own. A single person was not permitted to adopt children, and marrying a woman in my line of work was unseemly. Being a hooker, though, provided a means for me to adopt Emily."

"How'd you do it?"

"I didn't." She grinned. "People forget that powerful men visit hookers, and that gave us influence in a town this size," she said. "We compromised. Emily came to live with me for a spell, and no one concerned themselves with adoption papers. She stayed and no one asked questions. Too, Emily was a small, mute child, who exhibited special talents. Her skills scared the matrons at Bastard House. It frightened the other children, too. Sending her to live with me made everyone happy, especially me."

Natty moved around to the opposite side of the stone box. "I had to quit whoring, of course, but I had enough stashed away by then to make a comfortable home for me and Emily. Eventually I took in a couple more orphans, so Emily would have playmates, but she always kept to herself."

"The other children are the photographs on your piano?" Addison asked.

"That's right. My babies, the only family I ever had. Emily, though, was my first and the most special to me. We shared a bond. I convinced her that her unique gifts were what made her special, so she let me come into her secret world of silence and magic."

Natty's hands moved down her dress, smoothing the fabric. She removed a piece of paper from her pocket and took a deep breath. "Emily began to speak. She only talked when she had something important to say. Not a chatterer like me. She wrote a hell of a lot, though." She looked at Addison. "That's how I knew your name. The year she died, she wrote a poem about ... let me see if I can get it right from memory."

One soul soars, another swims,
An orphan's born of careless men.
Another comes when I am done,
Look for one named Addison.

"The poem goes on to talk about 'spiritous deeds' and something about a child lying on a stone floor in darkness, crying and losing her soul."

"Emily foretold that I would come here."

"Seems so, yes." Natty caressed the stone over Emily's coffin.

"How old was Emily when Stewie killed her, Natty?"

"Nineteen, in her prime. She looked older, mature and sophisticated. Beyond her years." Her head dropped. "That was all many years ago." She handed Addison the paper she'd taken from her pocket. It was a photograph of a beautiful girl with long, dark hair, who wore a sleeveless full-length dress, and was posed at the piano in Natty's home.

"Emily Mackenzie," Addison whispered to herself. "I think we've crossed paths."

272

Principal Keeper

Natty's lips tightened and she bit her lip. Addison stepped forward and placed her arm around Natty's shoulder.

Thunder rattled the metal door and the light bounced around the tomb. They were silent as the rumbles passed.

"Time to go," Natty announced, and wiped her face. "I have more to show you back home, important things that have been waiting a long time for you to visit." She turned again to Emily's casket. "Bye, bye, baby. Momma will see you again on Sunday." She kissed the stone and walked out of the crypt and locked the door behind them.

"Do you know someone named Daniel?" Natty asked as they drove through the flooded streets.

Chapter 44

The Crime Revisited

It would be hours before the storm passed and it wasn't safe to go outside. I was exhausted, emotionally and physically drained. I decided to rest while I could in the darkness of my room. Maggie insisted on sleeping with me. Both of us slept, even with the storm raging over the island.

I woke in the middle of the night. I heard Maggie growling. I saw her in the lightning flashes that came though the windows. She was at the foot of the bed, staring into the hallway. I rose and walked toward the door. I heard music. It was the familiar piano melody.

I stood at the top of the stairs. The room below was an ocean of blue light. The woman was there. She stared at me, and then moved up the stairs. Her eyes never waver from mine until she stood directly in front of me. She was crying. Her expression pleaded with me.

It was Caroline.

Principal Keeper

"I know you're Caroline," I said, but she didn't respond. "I know you died here on the island. How can I help you?"

The moment was surreal. I was talking to a poltergeist. She'd been dead for a long time. Was she a manifestation of my troubled mind? I wanted her to be real. I didn't believe in ghosts before coming to the island. Now a spirit stood inches away from me, her glaze locked on mine, and I spoke to her. It was an absurd moment.

She turned and drifted down the stairs, through the open door and into the storm. I followed her out into the rain with Maggie at my heels. Caroline's light passed through the door of the tower and disappeared.

I used the safety line to reach the door and opened it. The lower room was dark. In the lightning flashes, I saw a man seated several steps up on the spiral stairs. His shoulders were slumped and his face was buried in his hands. He stood, turned and started up the stairs. He wore boots, a wool cap, and a waistcoat over a wool sweater. He stopped near the top, placed something over his head, and disappeared. A thunderous voice, like the sound of the foghorn, resonated along the walls.

"Forgive me, Caroline. I meant you no harm." His words ended with a guttural, deep-throated moan.

When the lightning came again, I saw the man step over the railing and jump. There was a rush of air as he fell toward me, and then jerked violently. His limp body swung over the capstone. I heard the rope groan against his weight.

275

I was horrified at the sight of his distorted face. His swollen eyes forced his lids open and his tongue protruded from his lips. I stepped backward, stumbled and fell. It was then I saw the open well. Blue light radiated up from the hole. I crawled forward and looked inside. The woman stared up at me from the water. She reached out. I tied to take her hand. Our fingertips were inches apart, but she sank lower. Her eyes stayed open as her head went underwater. I stretched further, lost my balance and fell into the well. The lady was gone and the blue light receded with her.

I heard a baby crying above me. I looked up just as the stone lid began to close. I thought I saw a familiar face staring back at me. I grabbed the metal rungs and climbed. One rung, then another and only two more, then the lid closed tight. I reached the stone ceiling and pushed, but it was too heavy.

The water rose up my legs, then my chest, and then it was at my neck. I took deep breaths. I used the metal rungs to push myself deeper. My feet hit the bottom. It was dark and cold. I felt my way into the tunnel and swam toward the first cavern. I dug my fingers into the stones in the ceiling and pulled myself along. I fought back waves of fear and claustrophobia. I thought about childhood days when my friends and I challenged each other to see who could hold their breath the longest in the swimming pool. I never won the game.

When I felt I could no longer hold my breath, and my chest convulsed and my mind began to cloud, I bobbed to the surface in the first cave. I braced against the ceiling and raised my nose up into the pocket of air. I filled my lungs as best I could before the water rose higher. My hands clawed the walls and I felt metal. I sank to the floor and swam in what I thought was the direction of the larger room. The walls closed in around me. There was no escape. My lungs burned and I began to lose consciousness. I was dying. My last thoughts were of Addison and the moments we'd shared. I thought of my son, who would read of my death and never know his father. A familiar melody led me into darkness and sleep.

Chapter 45

The Aftermath

Gulls squawked and circled the tower. Waves lapped at the shore. It was the kind of new day meant to erase any memory of the night before.

There was evidence of the severity of the storm. Pools of water between the rocks, land-locked urchins and jellyfish, and kelp vines littered the courtyard. There was silence, and nothing moved except for the clouds, the waves, and the gulls. That was the scene, I learned later, until Maggie appeared and began to dig through the debris.

"Daniel!" a woman's voice called. Addison ran up the path, knelt beside me, and helped Maggie pull seaweed and driftwood from the pile. She saw my left hand and arm. They dug until they freed me. Addison told me later that I was unconscious. My hair was matted and my clothes were soaked with seawater. I had salt stains in the folds of my face and along my hairline.

Addison told me there was no response when she raised my head. She thought I was dead. "Oh, Daniel, you can't die. We've come so far. We have to see this through." She saw my hand move, and my eyes fluttered open. "Daniel?"

I was disoriented and the sunlight burned my eyes. I closed them again.

"Daniel, it's Addison." Maggie was barking. "Can you hear me?"

"Yes," I whispered. "I hear that noisy rock dog, too."

"Hush," I heard her scold Maggie, but it didn't silence her.

Addison told me later that it was then that she saw the young woman. She stood ten yards away, watching. Her hair was long and she wore a sleeveless dress. Behind her was another woman with Gibson styled hair. She was more mature and wore a full-length lace-trimmed blue dress. The two women turned and walked away.

I opened my eyes and struggled to sit up.

"Daniel, it's Caroline … and Emily."

I rose up on my elbow and looked in the direction that Addison pointed. I saw the two shadowy figures before they melted into the sunlight.

"That was the dark young woman I told you about," I told her and looked up into her face.

"Yes, I know," she said. "I know who she is now, but first things first. Everyone is searching for you down by the tower and cottage. This was the last place I saw you and Maggie, on this cliff, when you waved as I passed in the sailboat, so I thought to look for you here."

"Lucky for me," I said.

I struggled to stand, but my legs were shaky. I brushed sand from my clothes. My coat was missing. "I must have washed out of the mouth of the cave, and into the ocean. I don't remember. I blacked out."

"You were in the caves during the storm!"

"I fell in, you might say, and the lid closed, so I was trapped."

"How did you get to the top of the cliff?" she asked and looked over the ledge and down the rock wall to the waves below. "You couldn't have climbed up here if you were unconscious."

"I don't know, Addison."

"We'll figure it out later. Right now, let's get you back to the search party. The inspector keeps repeating that he's never lost a keeper on his watch. Let's go show him his record is intact."

There was the sound of metal against rock as I freed my ankles from the debris. Addison moved the kelp aside and exposed a bronze box incased in a thick layer of aged wax. She picked it up and held it in both hands. Etched on the top lid was 'Luke 21.32.'

Chapter 46

Lost Pieces – Two Months Later

"You're the principal keeper, aren't you?"

I'd just walked into the store. Maggie waited on the walk outside. My pantry was light, and I hadn't shopped since I drove up from the City.

"Say," the man behind the counter asked again, "aren't you the principal keeper of the harbor light?"

"A few months back, yes. Now I go out to inspect the facility, I explained.

"It were my boy who gave you that rock dog, the retriever out there." He pointed at the door.

"You're Cletus Bailey's father?"

"That's right, Cletus' my boy." I began to fill my basket. "What's the ministry plan to do about a keeper?"

"It's going the way of most lighthouses today, fully automated."

"So you won't be living out there no more?"

"No, but I'll visit from time-to-time. The ministry retained me part-time to check on things occasionally," I told him.

"What's the scuttle on rumors about ghosts and tunnels with caves, and all such things?"

"Just rumors, Mr. Bailey. It'd be romantic if it were true, I suppose, and good for the tourist trade if our harbor light had ghosts," I told him. "But, I know firsthand that it's quiet out there on the rock in the middle of the Bay."

"I figured as much," he grunted and wiped his nose with a handkerchief. "My old woman believes all that crap, but I know'd better when I first heard all those silly things."

"You're the wiser, for sure, Mr. Bailey," I told him.

He grunted, to put a period on our conversation, and then returned to his place behind the counter. I finished shopping and headed home.

***

I walked through the backdoor of the museum, into the kitchen, and dropped the bags onto the counter.

"Am I going to get some help with these groceries?" I called out.

"You're doing okay without me." Addison stood in the doorway.

Principal Keeper

"I crossed the room and took her in my arms. "So, this is how it's going to be? I do the shopping, and work?"

"And I do the cooking, only because I'm better at it. The museum matrons keep the house, with the exception of the private quarters upstairs. Working is your choice."

"I enjoy teaching economics," I told her, "until I produce my first best seller." I began to empty the bags. "Keeping the lighthouse is a breeze these days. Care to take a trip out tomorrow?"

"We just got back to Bellwether Bay last night, Daniel. Wouldn't you rather wait a couple days?"

"We could," I said.

"But we won't," she said and smiled. "Are you ready?"

"To return to the lighthouse? Sure," I said.

"No, I mean are you ready to hear the rest of the story?" she asked.

I'd been two months. Addison insisted that I needed time to heal, and she needed time to put the story together. She distracted me by encouraging me to journal about my experiences at Seward Lighthouse. She called it a "therapeutic exercise." We both had the idea of turning the story into a novel. I told her that journaling was easy, chronicling day-to-day experiences, but writing a novel was a beast. She said I had a great story to tell, and I told her I couldn't write it until she gave me the stuff she uncovered. I said I wanted to make it Emily's story, the daughter, but she insisted it was Caroline's. It had always been about Caroline, for Addison. She'd fantasized about Caroline's sad life and mysterious death from the first day she read the diary, so the story had to focus on the older woman, the mother. That was fair, given that our journey began with the mystery of what happened to Caroline and why she haunted the island.

"Can we be on the balcony, the tower gallery, enjoying lunch, when you tell me what you discovered?" I asked.

"Sure. That'd be fitting. We'll make the trip in the morning," she said.

***

I called and arranged for the launch. At first light, we sat on the dock waiting for our ride. The harbor was crowded with lobster boats. Harvest was good this year and the market price stayed high from the previous season. It would be a good year in Bellwether Bay.

I was on the rock three weeks ago, so this wasn't my first trip out since the storm. My duties were simple. I checked equipment, did general maintenance and repairs, made a quick pass through the house to make certain vandals hadn't been on the island, and collected debris. The capstone was sealed, so there was no access to the caves. I went to the top of the cliff, found my old stool, and ceremoniously tossed it into the sea.

Principal Keeper

This was the first trip that Addison and I took to the island together. She checked on the house, and I made the rounds. It was an easier job these days.

When chores were complete, we met at the tower door and went to the top. The chairs were still stacked inside the lamp room. We put them in the shade on the leeward side, away from the wind. Addison brought a lunch and a bottle of wine. We'd finished eating and were enjoying the view when we got down to the subject.

"If I'm going to do justice to the story in my novel, I need to know everything," I said.

"We know," she began, "that Colin thought he killed Caroline. We know from the diaries that he loved her, and admonished her for leaving the capstone open, because the open well was a danger to her baby. Emily wasn't his biological child, but he treated her like she was his own."

"Everyone will always believe that Colin murdered Caroline," I said.

"You're probably right, but I don't think it was intentional. Maybe he got drunk, forgot she was in the caves, and closed the lid to protect the baby." She sipped her wine and shielded her eyes to watch a sloop tack into the wind a hundred yards offshore. "We know that Caroline drowned in the rising tide beneath the island, and most probably her body washed out to sea. Colin's role in her disappearance is suspect. You and I know for certain that she was in the caves when the lid closed and trapped her in the rising water. My

285

time with Caroline's ghost when I was alone down there, and your harrowing drowning experience are evidence of that fact."

I filled our glasses. We rested back against the lamp house and watched the traffic in the bay. The view was like listening to music or reading great literature. There was no need for conversation, for filling voids, because there were none.

I understood, now, why people took to the sea, often alone, to find themselves and search for meaning in their lives. Surrounded by nature, experiencing it all, the ocean, the sky, the wind, gave purpose to existence. I lived at the will of nature, vulnerable to God's creations, and survived. I became one with the universe. It wasn't me that came to accept life at Seward Lighthouse, but rather it accepted me. That, in short, changed my life.

Addison, too, was part of the equation that saved my life. She was the compass that led me to find new purpose. She came to make the journey with me, and now she was part of the beauty of this place that was buried deep in my soul.

"There's more to share, Daniel," she said. "I learned that Emily wasn't taken to the orphanage right away. A Bellwether family took her in, and she lived with them for two years, until she was six. Her special skills probably scared the family in the same way she frightened staff and students at the orphanage."

"Who in Bellwether took in the child?" I asked.

"The family of Captain Jeremiah Woods," Addison said. "The museum. That's how mother got her hands on the diary." She handed me a photograph and asked, "Does she look familiar?"

"It's the woman by the windows in the inn. The same one at the piano and who visited the island." It hit me, then. "She was there when you found me on the cliff, after I washed out of the cave." I looked at Addison. "Who is she?" I asked.

"That's Emily, Caroline's child. She's nineteen in that picture." She paused and looked at me.

"That's impossible," I said. "Emily would be ..."

"... much older, yes, if she were alive," Addison said. "Emily died a few months after it was taken, in 1947. You're certain that it's the same woman you saw at the inn?"

I was confused, and struggled to pull my thoughts together. I never imagined that the dark lady was also a spirit. I'd seen her often, in so many places. I recalled, then, that others never noticed her. My question was why did she haunt me?

"How did she die?" I asked.

"Remember your dream about the woman crossing the street in New York City and being hit by a car? That actually happened."

"But, in my dream, she appeared to be floating, face down, and her clothes were wet. Why?"

Addison looked at the picture. "I think she was showing you how she died, and giving you clues about her mother's death." She turned her attention to the harbor. "The old woman in New York,

287

Natty, who adopted Emily, played a tune on her piano that she said Emily used to hum. Do you want to guess the tune? She taught Emily to play it."

My head was spinning.

"I have more to show you." She handed me a second picture. "Here's another one Natty loaned me. That's Emily, again, leaning on the piano. She's wearing the dress you described."

It was unquestionably the dark young woman that I saw repeatedly, on the island, at the piano in the ballroom, in the lobby next to the windows, and on the stair landing at the restaurant. It was Emily, but she hadn't aged in seventy years.

"How … ?"

"You know the answer, Daniel," she said. "There's only one way that the woman in that picture is the same person you saw in the village. And, from what you've told me, she played the same tune in the hotel ballroom. Did she ever speak to you?"

I realized I'd never heard her voice.

Chapter 47

My mind replayed all the memories I had since coming to the rock. It all made sense in a warped and surreal way. "Why didn't Emily haunt me here, in the storms, with Caroline and the old man?"

"She did haunt you here, but she didn't die here. She wasn't trapped on the island like her mother."

"Why did Emily haunt me at all?" I asked.

"Natty said Emily was special. She hardly spoke, but she could read at an early age. She probably read her mother's diary while she was in the Wood's home here in Bellwether. She must have known about her mother's overwhelming love for John, her father, and Caroline's deep sadness over his death. She may have even known how her mother died. When an unrequited lover killed Emily, her spirit set out to free her mother, and reunite her parents."

We turned our attention to the harbor. The wind picked up, but that favored the sailboats. They leaned deeper into the waves and rushed their tacks. It was fun to watch from our vantage point on the tower. The only sound was the wind and the gulls. We left Maggie at home in Bellwether, and I think the birds were looking for her.

They'd land on the balcony and stare up at us. It was more likely they were eyeing our lunch.

Addison had had time to work things out in her mind, but I was just now trying to process everything. It was all conjecture, of course. Neither of us understood the motives of restless spirits.

"She probably couldn't do it alone," Addison said, finally. "To free her mother's spirit, to reunite her parents, Emily needed your help. She needed to bring the living and the dead together."

She stood, and inched along the railing until she was several feet away, as though she was kindly leaving me alone to sort things out for myself. The light closed in around me. I felt my heart race and I was nauseous. I wanted it all to make sense, to have a thread of logic and reason. Spirits may have found peace, but now *my* thoughts were restless and searching for solid ground.

Addison explained that she never thought meeting me was a coincidence. She felt that I was key to finding out what happened at Seward from the moment we shook hands.

"Maybe it was wishful thinking, but I dreamt someone would solve the mystery, and you came. When I heard the lighthouse had a new keeper, and that he was a young man, I wanted to meet you."

Addison said she was attracted to me the first time we met, the day she visited the island. I told her that her life-long obsession with Caroline's love story prepped her for a romantic encounter. She punched my arm and then kissed me.

"You gotta' love a guy who's pursued by beautiful poltergeists," she said. "I have an advantage on Caroline and her daughter. I'm real."

"Yes, you are," I said.

Addison reminded me of the scripture copied in the diary, and written on the lamp glass and etched on the waxed box. Luke 21:32, *'Truly I say to you, this generation will not pass away until all things take place.'* She believed that Caroline would not rest until she found John again, and the only way that could happen was if John came to her.

"So Caroline thought I was her husband, John?" I asked. "I'm not John."

Addison moved further along the railing, and followed the shadow of the tower. "I think the story goes deeper," she said. "You were meant to find Caroline. Seward didn't have a keeper for a generation or two, and then circumstances brought you here. I think Emily used us to bring her parents together. We were meant to be here, right now. We're just a couple generations late."

I stood and stepped to the railing. I looked over the side and recalled the hours I'd spent here, surveying the island below and the ocean stretched out before me.

"I want to understand, Addison," I said, "but this is far fetched."

"Seeing ghosts isn't far fetched?" she asked. "Washing out of a cave, unconscious and ending up on top of a cliff isn't far fetched? How is what I'm proposing any more absurd?"

"Your theory suggests that we were born to fulfill Emily's wish, and to solve the mystery of Caroline's death."

Addison believed that Emily thought she contributed to her mother's death. Colin wouldn't have inadvertently closed the well over her mother if he didn't worry about Emily crawling into it. Emily somehow knew that her mother's spirit would never rest until the mystery of her death was solved, and she was reunited with John.

"Think about the notes Emily left behind with Natty," she said. "'Momma can't rest', she wrote. 'Got to bring Momma and Poppa together' was another one. They were prophetic ramblings, like her prophesy that I would come looking for her. That's how Natty knew me. Emily lived to fulfill that goal. It was a mission she carried with her to her death, to put an end to her mother's wanderings on this island."

I'd accept that my presence on the island may have stirred Caroline's spirit, but it would take time to believe that our journey to the lighthouse was predestined.

"I have one last item from the wax box to share with you," she said. "I need you to keep an open mind."

Chapter 48

She handed me one more photograph. It was tattered, the edges were black with age and wear, but the image was clear. It was a picture of Caroline's husband.

"This was the photograph that Caroline mentioned in her diary. It was a source of strength and comfort in moments of sadness and loneliness. It was also in the wax box. Look familiar?" she asked.

It was a picture of John, but I recognized immediately that it could be a picture of me, the person I'd become since coming to Seward Lighthouse. John was a robust man with sandy hair and sharp features. It was easy to imagine that he could have been a man of the sea. He could have been a lighthouse keeper.

I was speechless.

"Think of it this way," she said, "maybe it wasn't so much about reuniting souls, but about rekindling a light ignited by the union of two people who loved so deeply that death could not separate them forever. The light dimmed when John died, but Caroline wouldn't let it go out. She held on to her memories of him. Their union created Emily, who brought them back together. But Emily couldn't do it until her mother's spirit was released from the lighthouse. That's where you came in."

She moved closer and wrapped her arms around my shoulders. "You're not John," she said. "But, you helped Emily make things right again."

I would always struggle with my ghostly encounters at Seward Lighthouse and my connection with Caroline. Was her spirit free? Are she and John together, and with Emily? Would Addison and I be the only people who'd ever know the truth about the unwavering love between Caroline and John, and how Caroline died?

I eventually came to believe that spirits were put to rest and mysteries were solved. The unknown was now known, and souls torn apart were reunited. One could assume that what lingered for nearly a hundred years had moved on. Perhaps Addison and I would make a life together. If so, I was certain that the unnatural forces brought us together were gone.

It felt as though my otherworldly experiences were reduced to ashes and, as we learned, there's no life to be lived in the ashes.

Seward Lighthouse was quiet now. The caves beneath the island were sealed for at least for another generation. Everyone in the village knew the lighthouse was still out there on the horizon, and that anyone could see it, if the conditions were perfect and they knew where to look.

The End

Acknowledgments

I rarely write acknowledgements. Perhaps that's because the people who deserve acknowledgment are so obvious to me. There're family and close friends, and advisors, and proofreaders, and grandkids. They know who they are, and they know how grateful I am for their positive influence on my writing. Yes, grandkids have a lot to do with the success of my writing. Grandparents who read this will understand.

Sara Jackson warrants special mention because she's created nearly every one of the novel covers. She started out in my life as a friend and academic associate, and now she's just a very good friend who does beautiful work. So I value her, and her creative talent, very much.

I owe certain writers who came before me, who inspired and influenced my work. Writers like Ray Bradbury, Earnest Hemingway, Pearl S. Buck, David McCullough, Carson McCullers and J. D. Salinger. Some of them taught me style and form, and others taught me character development and mood, as well as the literary power of illusion. Kudos to Stephen King for writing a book titled *On Writing* that helped development my structure.

Writers are the only professionals I've met who can write for themselves, AND teach others their craft. Not all, but many have what Shakespeare deemed an unattainable skill: to do and to teach.

I'm reluctant to speak of personal associations that influence and motivate my writing. That information is too close to the rawness of who I am. My memoirs were enough folly cleaved from the core of my being to cause me nightmares, and to discourage me from offering further details of my personal life.

My greatest appreciation and acknowledgment is extended to my readers. Thank you. Love you all.

Made in the USA
Monee, IL
04 February 2021